"Is there something I can do for you, Agent Lama?"

Mitch seemed more muscular than before. His shoulders broader beneath the polo shirt that hugged them and the well-defined muscles of his chest. On his right arm was the tattoo that she had found undeniably sexy and dangerous when she had first discovered it. His hair was shorter, but framed the strong lines of his face better and brought attention to his eyes. Startling slate-gray eyes followed her every move.

"We need to talk, Dani."

"Talk? You have more from Lazlo about the mission?"

He released an exasperated sigh. "It's not about the assignment and you know it."

What she knew was that she was torn between having him take her into his arms and kicking his ass for breaking her heart.

Dear Reader,

When I was asked to write the story in which this heroine first appeared, *More Than a Mission* (August 2006), I was also asked to leave the status of "the Sparrow" in question. I was delighted! Why? Because I totally fell in love with the relationship between the two twin sisters, and because I knew there was more to Dani and the story of why she became "a world-renowned assassin." Since writing *More Than a Mission*, many readers have asked whether Dani was actually dead and also, how I could redeem Dani if she *had* killed or aided in the death of the Prince of Silvershire. I won't give anything away, but I hope that by the time you finish *Secret Agent Reunion,* you'll understand the demons that drove Dani and sympathize with the choices she made.

Why did I choose such a hard road for Dani? I see the news every day, and the toll that drugs take on our society is immense. I wanted to make a point that even recreational drug use comes with a price you may not see—the thousands of people who die as a result of drug-related activities, much like Lizzy Bee's and Dani's parents. I hope you'll enjoy not only this action-packed story, but also the romance between Mitch and Dani, since they have become two of my favorite characters.

Caridad

Caridad Piñeiro

SECRET AGENT
REUNION

Silhouette®

Romantic
SUSPENSE

SILHOUETTE BOOKS

ISBN-13: 978-0-373-27546-5
ISBN-10:   0-373-27546-3

SECRET AGENT REUNION

Books by Caridad Piñeiro

Silhouette Romantic Suspense

Darkness Calls #1283
Danger Calls #1371
Temptation Calls #1390
More than a Mission #1428
Secret Agent Reunion #1476

Silhouette Nocturne

*Death Calls
*Devotion Calls
*Blood Calls

*The Calling

CARIDAD PIÑEIRO

was born in Havana, Cuba, and settled in the New York metropolitan area. She attended Villanova University on a Presidential Scholarship and graduated magna cum laude. Caridad earned her Juris Doctor from St. John's University and became the first female and Latina partner of Abelman, Frayne & Schwab.

Caridad is a multipublished author whose love of the written word developed when her fifth-grade teacher assigned a project—to write a book that would be placed in a class lending library. She has been hooked on writing ever since. Articles featuring Caridad's works have been published in various magazines and newspapers. She has appeared on Fox Television's *Good Day New York,* New Jersey News' *Jersey's Talking* with Lee Leonard and WGN-TV's *Adelante Chicago.* Caridad was also one of the Latina authors featured at the first-ever Spanish Pavilion at the 2000 Chicago BookExpo America. Caridad's novels have been nominated for various readers' and reviewers' choice awards, including awards from *Affaire de Coeur,* Harlequin Books and RIO. *Danger Calls* was a 2005 Top 5 Read from *Catalina* magazine and the first book selected for *Catalina*'s cyber book club.

When not writing, Caridad is a mom, wife and attorney. Caridad also teaches various writing workshops and heads a writing group at a local bookstore. For more information on Caridad's books, contests and appearances, or to contact Caridad, please visit www.caridad.com.

This book is dedicated to all my wonderful nieces and nephews—Brendon, Deanna, Erika, Jonathan, Lauren, Peter, and Vincent—I love you all! You're the best.

Chapter 1

Only someone who had come back from the dead truly knew how deadly distractions could be.

Danielle Moore had let personal feelings get in the way of a top-secret mission over a year ago and had nearly lost her life. So she kept her eyes glued to the man—six feet two inches of thick muscle—as he charged at her like a linebacker after a quarterback, arms outstretched to trap her in his embrace.

Dani used his momentum against him, sweeping him aside with a matador like step. Turning quickly as he stumbled by, she snapped an elbow to the back of his neck and dropped him to the ground. Before she could totally incapacitate him, another more compact man charged at her from the opposite side of the room.

She pushed off the first man's fallen body and came up ready for action, but as she did so, something pulled along her midsection. A twinge of pain followed, but she tamped it down. She couldn't allow physical discomfort or weakness to divert her attention.

As the smaller man shoved past his rising friend, she released a sharp dropkick, catching him squarely in the chest and rocking him backward, where he immediately tripped over the larger man. Both men sprawled to the ground in a messy heap.

Dani stopped, placed her hands on her hips and laughed as they tried to untangle themselves and resume their attack.

"Come on, boys. Is that the best you can do?" she teased in fluent French.

After months of training together, the three of them had developed an easy camaraderie. Even now, when the men couldn't seem to contain Dani as her physical strength and martial arts prowess returned rapidly, they accepted her superior abilities good-naturedly.

Her current physical state was quite different from what it had been nearly three months ago, Dani thought.

After being shot and lingering in a coma off and on, she had emerged long enough to approve the removal of the bullet that had lodged precariously close to her spine. Three months after that, she had finally been well enough to begin physical therapy and try to get back into shape.

She had a new mission waiting for her, after all. At least, that's what the enigmatic man by her bedside had intimated to her so many months ago.

Dani now knew who that mysterious angel was—Corbett Lazlo, the elusive powerhouse behind the Lazlo Group, a private agency known for handling the most discreet and sometimes dangerous of missions. A group well known to her from her time with the Secret Intelligence Service, or SIS, the British equivalent of the CIA and the agency at which she had worked as the Sparrow, a world-renowned assassin.

Only she hadn't really been an assassin. All her supposed "kills" had been taken into SIS custody so that SIS might find out more information about an elusive crime organization they called SNAKE, which they suspected of being responsible for a number of illegal operations.

She had let her last mission get personal. Her actions had resulted in the death of the prince of Silvershire and had nearly caused her death and that of her twin sister. SIS had been less than pleased that, in her quest to find her parents' killers, she had messed up the mission in Silvershire, the small European island kingdom she had called home at one time. With her cover as the Sparrow possibly blown and an international incident brewing, SIS had tossed her out.

Lazlo, who had also been thrown out of SIS many years earlier, was the man she had to thank for keeping her alive. He was the one responsible for the medical treatment that had worked a miracle and brought her back from the dead.

He had taken her into his agency and told her that he would let her know when the time was right for her to be reborn and go out on another mission.

She felt mission-ready now and sensed that somehow Lazlo would know that.

He seemed to know everything about everyone while she, like most of the people she had met within his group, knew little about him. To her surprise, few had even seen the elusive Mr. Lazlo.

After thanking her two sparring partners for the training session, she walked to the gym to finish her workout. She took a place at the first station and lifted the weights, evenly pushing up the bars on the bench press and enjoying the strength she had regained in her arms. Satisfied, she finished her reps and moved on to the next station and then the next.

By the time she finished, her muscles trembled from her exertions, but it was a good feeling. The kind of sore that said she was getting stronger.

The kind of pain that confirmed she was still alive.

In the locker room, she peeled off her clothes and grabbed a towel, ready for a long soak in the Jacuzzi. As she passed a mirror, she stopped short, surprised by what stared back at her.

The image of a hard-bodied woman of average height was reflected in the mirror. Shoulder-length hair in need of a trim. Fine-boned shoulders leading to full breasts above a long, barely pink scar that ran down her middle. Beside the scar was the ragged, stellar-shaped wound where she had been shot during her last mission.

The physical wounds of the past year were alive in her vision, much like those in her heart, which had been there far longer. The scar of her parents' murder. The ragged and still unhealed wound from her lover's death barely three years ago.

Dani ran her hand down the long scar, but it was numb. Just as she was numb inside. Paralyzed. Yet she still had things to do so that might make her feel alive again.

So that she could finally go home. Go and see her twin sister, Elizabeth.

Only, as she'd heard before, she suspected that she could never truly go home again.

Lazlo agent Mitch Lama watched as Dani sparred with the two men in the gym.

Was she ready? he wondered tapping his lips with his index finger as Dani deftly handled the two much larger men.

The frailness from her injuries was gone, as was the pallor that had colored her skin for the many months she had been unconscious and battling for life. Months during which he had come to sit by her bedside, urging her to keep up the fight. Reading to her in hopes that she might hear his voice and return because they had things to settle between them.

Now she was back from the dead and he didn't know what to do with her. What to do about the lies she had told him for so long. Lies that had nearly cost him his life and hers.

She looked strong now. Presumably ready for action.

He had always admired Dani's physicality. Been intrigued by the strength beneath the seemingly fragile and feminine surface.

She was a warrior. A champion who was forever prepared to take up a cause and fight a wrong.

He both loved and hated her for being a hero.

For nearly three years, he had been waiting to see her. To talk to her again. To be able to touch her and have her know it was him.

To ask her why she had lied to him about who she was, even as he'd lain dying.

A loud beep came from his computer, notifying him that he had an urgent message from Corbett Lazlo. A second later, his phone rang and he had no doubt who would be on the line.

He shut down his access to the camera trained on Dani, immediately regretting the loss of her.

"Lama," he said, a tinge of annoyance in his voice that he had been pulled away from his surveillance.

Corbett Lazlo identified himself. "Did you get my message?"

"Hold on just one second, sir, while I open it," he said, the cadence and tone from his days in the military coloring his speech. He double-clicked to open the e-mail message Lazlo had forwarded and held his breath as he read it.

The message threatened with its simplicity.

Ready for Round 2?

"I'm assuming Cordez couldn't track the source of this message either?" He wondered why their top computer person was having such difficulty tracing the mysterious missives.

"You're correct. Plus, I have some other news."

He knew the news would be bad so he preempted Lazlo's report. "Another operative is down. I'm assuming the same MO as before?"

"Unfortunately, yes. His body was discovered not far from our Prague offices. Close-range shot to the head, just above the left ear. Hollow-point bullet. I've asked our various contacts to see if they have a record of any assassins with a similar MO but I suspect there may be quite a few."

Mitch considered the facts and sensed that the moment for waiting and watching had ended. Time for him and the Sparrow to join forces and discover who was behind the messages and attacks.

"I'm assuming that you want me to activate the Lazarus Liaison now, Mr. Lazlo."

Silence came across the line before Lazlo asked, "Do you think she's ready?"

He recalled the sight of Dani as she sparred. "I think she's physically ready, sir."

"Quite the political answer. And you? Are you ready? Physically? Emotionally?"

He'd be a liar if he said "yes," and so he provided the only answer he could.

"That remains to be seen, sir."

Lazlo's rare amused chuckle cut across the phone line. "Well, then. We'll activate the Lazarus mission sometime tomorrow. Be prepared for a joint briefing with the Sparrow in the afternoon."

He wanted to protest that it wasn't enough time but suspected that he could never have enough time to fortify himself to see her again. To face Dani down and deal with all the issues sure to exist between them.

But he had no choice. Corbett Lazlo had saved his life and Dani's. For that reason alone, he was honor-bound to do what Lazlo was asking of him.

He only hoped that, when it was all over, he would finally have some peace in his life.

Chapter 2

Dani stared intently at the long steps leading up to Sacre Coeur on top of Montmartre. Months earlier she had tried to climb those steps but failed, her body debilitated thanks to too much time in bed. For the past few months she'd pushed herself by making each day's walk longer than the one before. Her hikes eventually brought her back to the bottom of these steps, but she had never felt strong enough to make the climb.

Until today.

She began slowly, pacing herself in the August heat, but about halfway up she knew.

She increased her pace and although she was slightly winded at the top, she made it. For a *Rocky*-like moment, she wanted to pump her arms in the air and jump around, but contained herself. She didn't want people to look at her and think, *Crazy Tourist*.

Instead, Dani glanced at Paris, laid out before her in all its splendor. From high up on Montmartre, most of the city and the Seine were visible on the clear summer day.

She paused to enjoy the sight for only a moment, knowing that she had not only pushed her physical limits, but that she had stretched the boundaries of how long she had been away from the Lazlo medical compound. The beep that sounded at her side a second later confirmed it.

Grabbing her cell phone, she read the text message—her presence was demanded back at the compound immediately. Mr. Lazlo wanted to meet with her.

It would take her time to walk back, and she sensed from the curtness of the message that she shouldn't dawdle. Texting back that she would be there within the half hour, she rushed back down the steps and walked to one of the side streets until she hit a main thoroughfare, where she quickly snagged a cab.

In French as flawless as her English, she asked to be taken to the Louvre and then she held on as the cab sped off, weaving through traffic and the assorted circles at a break-neck pace. When the cabbie stopped with a screech before the museum in record time, she mumbled a thanks to God for arriving in one piece and paid the man.

Racing past the pyramid, she walked to the bridge near the Seine, down the stairs to the riverbank and hurried to the metal grate beneath the bridge. Once she felt confident that it was secure, she used a specially encoded magnetic card to enter the tunnel and rushed toward the elevator to the Lazlo medical compound. After clearing the palm print and retinal scan, she proceeded to the main level of the compound where Jacques, the larger of her two sparring partners, waited for her.

"Mr. Lazlo asked me to bring you to his conference room as soon as you arrived," Jacques said in French with a polite bow.

"Of course," she replied and followed Jacques to a wing

of the compound she had yet to enter, wondering about the elusive Mr. Lazlo, whom she had met only once.

As he stopped at a door, Jacques placed his palm on another reader and with the same almost silent *whoosh*, opened the portal. "We've coded this door to allow you entry as well," he added as he motioned for her to enter.

"*Merci*," she said and walked in, expecting him to follow her into the lushly appointed conference room. Instead, the door closed silently behind her, leaving her alone in the space.

A large mahogany table filled the center of the area. Three of the walls were lined with matching bookcases, ornately trimmed with hand-worked moldings and filled with expensively bound leather volumes. An exceptionally large plasma monitor was mounted on one wall, and as she walked farther into the space, the lights dimmed slightly and the monitor snapped to life.

"Good afternoon, Dani. I trust you enjoyed your stroll this morning." The voice came from a speaker phone in the center of the table.

Dani had heard the voice only about a half dozen times since that one fateful meeting by her hospital bedside, but it was familiar enough for her to recognize.

"Good afternoon, Mr. Lazlo. Given your message, I had hoped to be meeting with you in person," she said as she strolled around the room, searching for whatever kind of surveillance equipment was being used to keep an eye on her.

"In time. But for now there is a matter of some urgency that requires your attention. That is, if you're ready for a mission."

"Not that I've minded your hospitality, Mr. Lazlo, but for months now I've been trying very hard to understand why you would want me to work for you." As she spoke, Dani walked around the room, searching for the location of the hidden camera.

"I know what it's like when SIS turns its back on you. I used to be one of them." A dead tone filled his voice at the admission, causing a sympathetic sensation within her. She still felt dead inside.

"I'm surprised you feel you can rely on me. My instincts have been rather bad lately."

"You believed the prince when he said he wasn't using drugs anymore, correct?"

Dani dredged up the memories of that night from her last mission. Normally she would have turned over the prince and the man who had hired her to kill him—Silas Donovan—to SIS to handle, but Donovan had dangled an intriguing bit of info before her. Donovan had insisted that the prince knew who had murdered her parents nearly a decade earlier.

Dani had wanted that information badly. So badly that she had put her personal quest above the SIS mission.

"Dani?" Lazlo prompted at her prolonged silence.

"I didn't think the prince would use the tainted cocaine I left behind that night," she finally admitted, still feeling guilty that she had played a part in Prince Reginald's death. She had believed he was clean and had hoped that having seen the error of his ways, he would reveal the names of those who had sold him drugs and possibly killed her parents.

She walked to the front of the room and paused before the plasma monitor. As she tracked her gaze along the sides of the bookcase beside it, she caught a telltale glint, almost like a speck of glitter against the dark wood. As she raised her finger to cover what she suspected was a fiber-optic camera, the image of her doing so appeared in the large monitor.

"Your admission of that is a good start. So, are you ready for an assignment?" Lazlo pressed again.

She nodded, and Lazlo began his report. "I need you to concentrate on the data I'm about to provide."

With a curt bob of her head to acknowledge the request, Dani seated herself at the table in a comfy leather library chair. Immediately, a picture of Silas Donovan came onto the screen.

"You're aware that Mr. Donovan paid them to assassinate the prince so Donovan's nephew could instead inherit the throne of the European principality of Silvershire."

As her gaze locked with that of the man in the photo, she remembered those cold eyes staring at her from behind his ski mask as Donovan had stood by, waiting for her to die after he had shot her. "Tell me something I don't know, Mr. Lazlo."

"We believe someone at SIS, or possibly even someone highly placed in the government sector with access to SIS, leaked information about you to the crime syndicate you were sent to infiltrate."

Dani considered his comment but shook her head in denial. "You think someone official blew my cover as the Sparrow?"

"It makes sense that once the syndicate knew you were SIS and knew your family history, they would naturally ask you to take on the job for Mr. Donovan. They knew you had a score to settle about your parents."

"And then they revealed my personal information to Donovan so he would eliminate me after I'd done all the dirty work? That's quite convoluted."

"Quite, my dear. But once your cover was blown, the crime bosses needed you gone and Donovan most likely wanted you silenced so you couldn't reveal his role in the prince's death."

Dani mentally ran through all that had happened and unfortunately, the facts supported the unlikely scenario. Painfully, she acknowledged that she had possibly been betrayed by one of her own.

"What does all of this have to do with the mission you want me to undertake?"

"There have been a series of recent incidents—"

"What kind of incidents?" she challenged, annoyed by the obtuseness of Lazlo's comments—until a series of photos flashed onto the monitor and Lazlo identified each of his murdered operatives.

"The last two have a similar MO—a close range shot to the head, just above the left ear, with a hollow-point bullet."

"The killer is issuing a challenge to you that he can get close anytime he'd like," Dani advised. "So that makes three operatives down in less than two months. Quite a personal attack on the Lazlo Group."

"More than you can imagine," he said in a way that raised the hackles on the back of her neck.

"We believe the first incident—which actually would make it four operatives attacked—may have occurred nearly three years ago. Different MO from all three of these kills, but the goal was the same—to disrupt an important Lazlo Group operation."

"Which was?" Dani asked, although in her gut she suspected what Lazlo would say even before he spoke or flashed the smiling picture of her dead lover up on the screen.

"Mitchell Lama. On assignment in Rome when he was knifed by a courier working for the syndicate. The courier you later turned over to your handler at SIS, but reported as killed to your contact at the crime organization."

Anger erupted within her, creating a chill in her gut. A chill that would only be removed by finding out who had set Mitch up and by making sure they were punished. Fighting off the violence that rose in her, because she knew she couldn't let it get personal again, she jumped out of the chair and stalked to one side of the room, hopefully out of range of the ever-intrusive camera.

"All roads lead to Rome, my dear. It's where these troubles possibly began. I need you to work with another Lazlo operative to find the SIS leak. We believe the information from that SIS leak is being used against the Lazlo Group."

"I'll find the leak, Mr. Lazlo. So who is this operative you want me to partner with?" she said, arms wrapped tightly around her waist as she struggled to contain herself.

The door *whooshed* open behind her, and she faced the tall, broad-shouldered man who entered.

She went completely still. Then a cold pit of rage formed in her gut. The numbness that had filled her center for months was swiftly replaced with a tight knot of pain.

She walked up to Mitchell Lama and punched him, snapping his head back with the force of her blow.

"You son of a bitch. You're not dead."

Chapter 3

Mitch was not about to let Dani land the second blow. He encircled her fist, stopping her jab mid-swing and, for good measure, snared her other hand. Not that his actions would necessarily stop Dani if she wanted to exact additional punishment. He'd seen her in action and knew she could hurt him if she still desired.

But she didn't desire more, it seemed.

Instead, she rose up on tiptoe and whispered, "Why didn't you tell me?"

Why? It seemed like such a simple question and yet…

"I lay dying in your arms and you couldn't confess the truth." His tones were low in the hope that the assorted bugs in the room wouldn't pick up the exchange.

"The truth? That I was the Sparrow? We worked too hard to manufacture that identity, no matter how much I wanted to tell you the truth," she shot back, inching higher on her tiptoes to get right up in his face and hiss the words.

"The truth is that your actions led to the death of Prince Reginald and nearly got my old partner and your sister killed," he replied calmly, anger at the deception she had perpetrated for the year that they had been lovers making him want to hurt her the way she had hurt him.

In front of his eyes her spirit deflated. She yanked her wrists from his grasp and stalked back to the table, where she plopped into one of the leather library chairs. It creaked and rocked for a second before she stilled its motion and said in a much louder voice, "You can't expect Mitch…Agent Lama and I to carry out this mission. We can't work—"

"You can, Dani. You have no choice. SIS believes that both you and Mr. Lama are dead. You've fallen off their radar, and so…"

"You basically have two highly experienced agents with new identities that no one will be expecting," Mitch confirmed. He walked to the table and took a seat opposite Dani.

"Exactly. Like Lazarus, the two of you are risen again for this assignment. After it is completed, I will assist you so that you may do whatever you want. For now, however, I need you to find out who is behind these attacks," Lazlo said, and since they apparently had no say, he continued with his report on the background of the operation.

"As I mentioned, all these troubles appear to have started in Rome. After recovering from his wounds, Agent Lama indicated to me that he had suspicions that someone within our group was also possibly leaking information."

Dani shot Mitch a quick glance, then looked at the speaker as she asked Lazlo, "Why the suspicions?"

Irritation made Mitch snap. "I am here, you know. You *can* ask me."

Dani faced him and laid her hands on the surface of the table. "So, Agent Lama. What clued you to a possible problem within your organization?"

"Besides getting gutted?"

Her fingers tensed on the tabletop, and a frown flashed across her features before she restrained her emotions. Had it possibly been concern he had seen for a moment? he thought before he continued.

"My partner, Aidan Spaulding, and I had been trailing Kruger, who your crime organization—"

"SNAKE," Dani jumped in.

"SNAKE?" Mitch asked, confused by the name.

A wry smile swept across her full mobile lips as Dani replied. "Sorry. It's an inside joke at SIS. We called them SNAKE for short—Syndicate of Nasties, Assassins, Killers and Evildoers."

"So, that old SNAKE acronym is still alive and well?" Lazlo asked. "In my day it stood for something else. I assume it still refers to the old Dumont family group?"

Mitch also chuckled. "SNAKE. I like it. Who are the Dumonts?"

"We believe Maximilian Dumont ran the crime organization for years. He recently passed away and we're not sure who is calling the shots now. My job was to infiltrate and identify the current power, plus try to get the goods on them," Dani explained.

"SNAKE and the Dumont family go way back," Lazlo said. "I had a run-in with the family years ago. With the son and daughter."

With a nod, Mitch continued with his earlier explanation. "So Aidan and I were trailing Kruger—the SNAKE courier—

because a Lazlo client believed that his competition was illegally selling conflicts diamonds, which Kruger was transporting. We reported Kruger's location to Lazlo. When we went to take him, however, Kruger was already on the run."

"Someone from SNAKE gave me his location. SNAKE hired the Sparrow to eliminate him because he'd ripped off one of their clients," Dani added, surmising that Kruger's whereabouts had come courtesy of the Lazlo Group leak.

Mitch didn't need to say that it had also allowed Dani to find him in one of the side streets leading away from Kruger's hideout after he had been knifed and left for dead.

"SNAKE's knowledge of Kruger's location just supports Agent Lama's theory that someone in our group may have leaked the information either to SNAKE directly or to someone at SIS. It's possible the Lazlo leak also provided information related to the Silvershire affair as well," Lazlo jumped in. "I can see already that bringing the two of you together will be quite helpful in discovering what's going on."

"We need to somehow interrogate Kruger," Dani said, and Mitch agreed with a nod.

"That may be difficult. First of all, everyone believes you're both dead and I don't want to reveal your existence at this time. Second, SIS may not be willing to allow anyone from our organization to interview him."

"Kruger is Ground Zero as far as we know, Corbett. If we can identify his contacts over the course of those few days, we may be able to determine who was feeding him information," Mitch advised and watched as Dani seconded his assertion with a quick bob of her head.

"Mitch and I can assume different identities for the briefing. Plus I'm sure that a man with your connections can arrange for a short interrogation," Dani added, her tones saccharine.

Silence came across the speaker. Then, "You and Elizabeth are quite alike, Dani. She said much the same thing to me some time ago. I'll see what I can do."

The plasma monitor shut off as did the phone connection, leaving Mitch staring at Dani across the width of the conference room table. It might be only four feet, but he knew that the chasm between them was much greater than that.

"Are you prepared to work on this assignment together?" he asked, unable to read much into her body language and facial expression.

Dani slowly rose from the chair, her gaze trained on him as if she was actually contemplating refusing the mission. But then her green eyes darkened, and a grim smile came to her face.

"I let something personal interfere with my assignment once before. It not only nearly cost me my life, but my sister's. I won't let that happen again."

Mitch didn't know how to react to the statement. That there was still something personal between them—something that could still bother her—was clear. That she thought she could shove it aside rankled.

What bothered him the most, however, was that he still cared what she thought and how she felt after her year of lies. After discovering, as he had lain dying, that she was the Sparrow.

Needing to build his own defenses, he nodded and slouched back in his chair, trying to seem disinterested as he said, "Who says anyone wants it to get personal again?"

Miserable, cold-hearted bastard, Dani repeated with each jab, punch and kick as she pounded the heavy bag in the gym, working out her frustration over the earlier meeting with Mitch.

Miserable, deceiving, *alive* son of a bitch, she thought, as with a final punch, she sank down onto the mat and leaned against the wall. Bringing her knees up tightly to her chest, she wrapped her arms around them, buried her head there and began to weep.

Mitch was alive.

How many times in the three years since his "death" had she wished for just that thing? Wished that they might have had a chance at a life together? A life without SNAKE and guns and violence and death.

How many times had she pictured the two of them, living in Leonia in a home near her sister, Elizabeth, whom she fondly called Lizzy Bee. Children running around them along the gardens and shore much as she and her sister had done before their parents' deaths.

She wasn't sure such a life was possible for her now. Maybe it never had been, she thought, and swiped at a tear only to scratch the skin of her cheek with the exposed edge of the Velcro along the wrist of the boxing gloves she still wore.

She snagged the edge of the glove's wrist-wrap with her teeth while drawing a shuddering breath and pulled it open. Then, she tucked the glove under her arm and removed its partner.

As she stood she swiped the remnants of the tears staining her face and vowed not to cry again over the things she couldn't change. Tears hadn't brought back her parents. They hadn't brought back Mitch....

Well, at least they hadn't brought back Mitch during the three years when she had cried for him regularly. But now...

The door to the training room opened, and Mitch walked in.

Dani hurriedly dashed away the last of her tears, turned and executed a series of bare-handed blows against the heavy bag, although not as powerfully as before due to the absence of the gloves. The last thing she needed was to break something, she thought, watching Mitch's approach from the corner of her eye.

When he stood about a foot away, hands tucked into the pockets of his tight jeans, she asked, "Is there something I can do for you, Agent Lama?"

She never broke the rhythm of her routine, nor directly faced him, and yet there wasn't a thing about him that didn't register.

He seemed more muscular than he had before. Bigger. His shoulders broader beneath the polo shirt that hugged them and the well-defined muscles of his chest. On his right arm was the intricate tribal tattoo that she had found undeniably sexy and dangerous when she had first discovered it beneath the elegant suits and clothing that Mitch generally wore.

His hair was a trifle shorter around his ears, but longer up top and stylishly gelled into slightly punkish spikes that brought out the sun-streaked highlights mixed in with the brown.

Again, not as elegant as the haircut she had known him to wear, but she liked this one more—it framed the strong lines of his face better and brought attention to his eyes. Startling slate-gray eyes that were following her every move and darkening with what she suspected was annoyance.

"We need to talk, Dani."

"Talk?" She shot the bag a punch, slightly harder than the ones before, and faced him. "You have more from Lazlo about the mission?"

Mitch released an exasperated sigh. "It's not about the assignment and you know it."

What she knew was that she was torn between easing against him and having him take her into his arms and kicking his ass for breaking her heart.

She did neither.

Instead, she crossed her arms and inched her chin up a

bit—not that by doing so she would make much of an impact. At six-foot three, Mitch had quite some inches on her average height as well as at least one hundred pounds more of muscle.

"I believe that you said you didn't want it to get personal again, Agent Lama."

"I don't," he replied curtly and then dragged a hand through his hair, making the spikes even more pronounced.

Pulling one hand from his pocket, he held it out palm up in a pleading gesture and leaned toward her to emphasize his point. "There's a lot that went on between us. Some good. Some very good. But a lot really bad as well."

Truthful, if not a bit blunt, Dani thought as Mitch went on.

"Whatever it was is in the past. Now we're partners. I need to be able to trust you to watch my back. You probably need the same from me."

A reasonable request, and even though what she was feeling toward him right now was major dislike, possibly bordering on hate for his deception, she had always intended to watch his back. That he had thought otherwise just added to her pique.

"I'm a professional, Mitch. Like it or not, you are my partner. I will guard your back, and I expect that you will guard mine."

He straightened away from her then and tucked his hand back into his pocket. With a shrug of those broad, thickly muscled shoulders, he said, "Right."

He stood there for a few seconds more, seemingly unsure of what to do next, until he yanked his hand back out of his pocket and thrust it out to her, as if to seal the deal.

"So, then, we're partners," he said, and, at her delay, gave a little shake of his hand as if to urge her on.

She looked at that hand and then up to his face, where

myriad emotions played across his normally neutral features. Neutral because, as secret agent types, they couldn't afford to allow their emotions to show to the enemy.

But as she shook his hand, his emotions were clearly etched on his face for her to see. Confusion. Regret. Desire, banked well behind the other two.

The handshake that lasted longer than it should have confirmed the final emotion wasn't just on his part, and they both abruptly pulled away from the handshake.

Dani rubbed her palm and the back of her hand, almost as if she could wipe away the remnants of the one disturbing emotion that had been communicated with a simple handshake. With a curt bob of her head, she confirmed the agreement. "Partners, but that's it." She tucked her chin down and walked out of the gym.

Chapter 4

Troy Dumont sat back in his chair and took a sip of the Johnnie Walker Blue in his glass. The taste of the scotch was smooth but with some bite as if to remind him that it was older than he was.

Months shy of twenty, he had nevertheless seen more of the world than most others his age. Done more than most, including killing a man. How else did you learn to run one of the world's largest crime syndicates if not by getting your hands dirty every now and then?

Although he had never met his grandfather, Maximilian Dumont, he hoped that he had inherited some strength from the man who had gone from being a mercenary to building a worldwide empire of assassins, gun smugglers and other assorted criminals.

Troy wanted to show his mother, who had inherited control of the syndicate after her brother's and father's deaths, that he could one day run their organization as well.

Taking another sip, he considered his mother as she paced back and forth while talking on the phone. A very important call had come in from one of their informants, interrupting their after-dinner conversation.

Annoyance flared through him at how often work pulled his mother away. How, for most of their lives together, one thing or another had always managed to interfere—although he understood just how much control was necessary to maintain power over such a vast network of bad asses. Control that his family kept in a number of ways, including elimination of anyone who got in the way—like Corbett Lazlo and his annoying band of do-gooders.

In the past few months his mother had grown more determined, almost fanatically so, to rid herself of the Lazlo Group. Lazlo's well-known agency had been a thorn in their side for quite some time, but lately, the Lazlo Group activities had managed to create even more problems for them. He didn't think the Lazlo Group had been smart enough to figure out the various sources of the Dumonts' illegal gains, but recently they had unwittingly slowed the flow of money from different operations.

"*Fils de pute,*" his mother, Cassandra, nearly screeched and he shifted forward in his chair, determined to find out what had set her off.

"Find out what Lazlo wants with Kruger and where he's taking him," she said as she reached one end of the room and whirled, then paced back to the other side, her long legs carrying her back and forth swiftly. Her slender body vibrated with anger.

"I don't care how difficult it will be. You're well paid to get this information for us." Her French accent intensified in tandem with her anger.

Her green eyes narrowed to tight slits as she shot him a glance. Realizing she had her son's full attention, she sent him an apologetic smile.

As the person on the other end of the conversation signed off, she snapped the cell phone shut, dragged a hand through the long, wavy strands of her auburn hair and walked toward him, the lines of her body elegant. Graceful. Dangerous.

"*Je suis si désolée, chéri.* Something unexpected came up." She cradled his jaw and stroked the line of it, her hand smooth against his skin. A mother's gentle touch.

He leaned into it and covered her hand with his, needy for her affection. She was all he had in the world, having never known the rest of his family. Grandfather. Uncle. Father. All dead before he could meet them. "It's fine, Maman. I just wish…"

Troy didn't have to finish. Cassandra seemed to know just what he wanted.

"Once this is done, *mon fils*, we'll have more time together."

He had heard her say it before, and, in general, she had kept her promises to him. For as long as he could remember, she had juggled the demands of the syndicate with those of motherhood in order to give him her attention.

When he had become old enough to learn about the business, she had begun to teach him much as her father had taught her and her brother.

Corbett Lazlo had been responsible for his uncle's death, and so he could understand his mother's current desire to see the Lazlo Group suffer. In their world, payback was common. Almost demanded. You didn't survive if you let others tread all over you.

But this ongoing vendetta with Corbett Lazlo was getting…tiring.

"You're losing sight of the bigger picture when it comes to Lazlo."

She pulled her hand away and walked to the bar, poured herself a drink. When she sashayed back toward him, she said, "You can't understand—"

"I know he killed your brother." He downed the last of the scotch, wincing as the burn worked down his throat.

His mother sipped her drink and considered him over the rim of her glass before she said, "It's more complicated than that."

He shot to the edge of his chair, placed his hand on her arm and applied gentle pressure to lower her glass. "So tell me why you want to hurt Lazlo so badly."

"He's disrupted our financing."

"*Merde*. You sent the Sparrow after Kruger because he was stealing from us. We needed a new courier anyway."

"That operative in Prague—"

"Would have taken forever to figure out how that organization was funneling us the money. This is about something else." But as his gaze met his mother's, he realized she was not about to reveal what drove her lately. What had been compelling her for the past three years and invading their time.

"When you're ready, Maman. I'm sure you'd tell me if it was something I should know."

"I would, *mon coeur*," she said. She cradled his cheek again and leaned forward, kissed his forehead. "I promise you, Troy. This has nothing to do with you."

When Dani had been an agent with SIS, they had footed the bill for an apartment in Rome close to the Villa Borghese. It had been home base for her when she wasn't traveling the world, capturing bad guys in her disguise as the Sparrow. During her non-spy times, she would "work" at the offices of a financial services company located not far from the Coliseum. The company provided a front for the local SIS headquarters and agents.

She had met Mitch years earlier at a bar not far from those offices. The attraction had been physical at first. Mitch's size and good looks had immediately snagged her attention. But after a few hours in his company, she had liked his humor and forthrightness.

During the dates that followed whenever he was in Rome, Mitch had mentioned that he worked for a private investigations firm and needing to be careful, she had used her SIS connections to confirm that he was employed by the Lazlo Group. She had also seen his military records and realized that behind the good looks and elegant clothing was a bona fide hero. Not that Mitch had ever bragged about his Silver Star or Purple Heart.

For the next year, she had come to learn more about the complex man he was and had fallen in love.

Now they were back in Rome together, but the Lazlo Group had decided she and Mitch would stay a good distance away from either of her old locations as well as the Lazlo Group office while they were on their mission.

The Albergo Santa Carmela hid on a small street in Rome's Trastevere section, painfully close to the spot where she had found Mitch bleeding to death nearly three years earlier. One part of her didn't understand why someone would chose a location bound to stir the emotional pot for both her and Mitch. Another part of her—the spy part—acknowledged that as a base of operations, the tiny hotel was close to perfect.

The street on which it was located had defied discovery even to locals, and the hotel boasted only twenty rooms, all on one floor and opening into a central courtyard. Easy to secure and with quick access for escape. If there was anything that made the hotel not perfect, it was the rather solicitous and eager staff, who had too many questions and paid too much attention to the supposed newlyweds checking in for a two-week stay.

Dani pasted a smile on her face as Mitch encircled her waist and with a playful wink, confirmed their status to the older woman behind the front desk. "Yes, that's right. We're on our honeymoon, so I hope you'll understand if the Do Not Disturb sign is on the door often."

The woman tittered and handed Mitch two keys for the room. "*Non lei disturbano, mai* you do not want to miss seeing *la citta eterna,*" the clerk replied, wagging a pudgy finger in emphasis.

Mitch friskily jostled Dani before bending his head and nuzzling her cheek. "Oh, we'll see the *la citta* eventually."

What she wanted to do was give him a shot to the ribs, but decided a different punishment would be better. She turned and whispered against his lips, "Eventually, *amore,*" and kissed him to shut him up.

Like most rash actions, it backfired on her as Mitch returned the kiss, leaving no doubt about just how well he could kiss and how it still affected her. She was soon clinging to his shoulders and opening her mouth against his until the excited squeal of the hotel clerk ripped them apart.

"*Il amore* will soon have the *bambini* for you."

Mitch coughed and shifted back a bit from her. "Not yet, *signora.* I'm not ready to share my wife with anyone."

The look he shot her made her pulse race, but she tamped down her unwanted desire. Taking the keys from the surface of the front desk, she motioned with them to one of the side exits. "The room is…"

"*A la sinestra,*" the clerk advised.

"*Grazie, signora*," she said and quickly turned left toward the room, wheeling behind her the modest-sized bag with her clothes and equipment. Mitch followed, a decidedly bigger suitcase trailing behind him.

Dani had chuckled when she had first seen the bag, which confirmed to her that Mitch's status as clotheshorse was intact. When they'd been together, no matter where they went or what the occasion, Mitch had always been sartorially splendid.

So unlike her usual dress when she had worked for SIS. At her home base, she kept to staid, dark business suits and mannish tailored shirts, which fit her cover as a financial services advisor. While on a mission as the Sparrow, she would tone down her appearance even further, going so far as to wash a dark brown rinse into her hair to kill the auburn highlights. The clothes she wore while on an assignment were likewise dark and drab so as to not attract attention.

It had been that lack of color combined with the calling card she left behind at her "kills"—a small bundle of feathers tied together with black ribbon—that had earned her the moniker of the Sparrow. The manufactured identity and faked assassinations had allowed her to infiltrate SNAKE, but only for a few jobs and not deeply enough to confirm who was behind the group, despite SIS's belief that the Dumonts were the masterminds of the organization.

When they entered the room, a large fruit-and-cheese basket and a bottle of wine sat on a long table to one side of the space. Dani walked over and pulled a card from the gift, smiled as she saw who it was from.

"Your Uncle Corbett wishes us the best on our honeymoon."

Mitch came to her side and took the card from her hand. "My uncle is such a thoughtful guy," he said with a grin.

Dani carefully unwrapped the cellophane from the basket, just in case it wasn't really from the Lazlo Group, but as she did so, Mitch leaned in close yet again. Too close.

"Honey, do you mind if I check my e-mails while you unpack?"

She glared at him as possibly an annoyed newlywed wife would, although she realized what he really planned to do. "Promise me this will be the last time, sweetie. It is our honeymoon, after all."

"Promise." He dropped a kiss on her cheek. She shot him what she hoped would look like a playful nudge if anyone was actually watching them.

Mitch pulled a PDA from a case on his belt and while seemingly reading his e-mails, slowly paced around the room, checking it for bugs the way any good agent would. Especially in a case like this, where they didn't know who in their organization might be working against them.

Dani watched him out of the corner of her eye as she examined the fruit basket. The top was, as expected, a collection of luscious fruits—peaches, figs, pears and grapes. The fruit, however, rested on some kind of platform in the basket. She wouldn't pull it out to examine what was beneath until Mitch had cleared the room.

"Almost done, sweetcheeks? I'm ready to check out this nice bed," she said, the tones of her voice sultry. As if to prove her need, she took a running step toward the king-sized bed in the middle of the room and launched herself onto its surface.

Mitch swung the modified PDA around one last time, but the unit didn't register that there were any listening devices or cameras in the hotel room. It was clear. He turned his attention to the bed. Dani rolled around on its surface, doing a fair imitation of a flounder out of water rather than a needy newlywed. Not that that kept him from imagining just how things might be if she were ready for him.

Like she had been after that kiss at the front desk.

He had promised her to not make it personal. To keep to just being partners, but sweet Lord, he hadn't expected it would be so damn difficult so damn fast.

He had forgotten just how Dani could affect him, even when she was being a total boob as she was now.

Which only made him want her more. It had been the same way when he had first met her nearly four years ago. He'd been intrigued by her bravado when she had approached him. Drawn by her beauty. But what had made him fall in love with her had been her complex nature—the mysterious side, which hid secrets behind her intense green eyes, and the goofy one she was now exhibiting as she flopped around on the bed's surface.

Walking over to the bed, he stared down at her, a smile on his face. She met his gaze and stopped her movement. "Everything okay?"

He could have lied and jumped her bones on the bed. Taken the moment to sample another kiss and the enticing press of her body against his.

But he couldn't do it. It would only cause more problems between them, and resurrecting old passions was the last thing either of them needed. When this mission was done, they had to go their separate ways. Like Lazarus, they might have both risen from the dead, but that didn't mean their love had also come back to life. How could it, when it had been a love based on deception—on both their parts.

"All clear."

At his comment, she flew from the bed back to the fruit basket, confusing him until she lifted out the fruit.

He approached, and they both looked down into the bowl of the basket, which was filled with DVDs and a portable USB drive. Judging from its size, one that could hold hundreds of gigabytes. He reached for one of the DVDs, but at the same time, his PDA rang.

The caller ID didn't list who it was, but both he and Dani knew.

"Good morning, Mr. Lazlo."

"Good morning, Mitch. I trust you and Dani had a nice flight on the corporate jet. Are the accommodations to your liking?" Lazlo said, the tones of his voice smooth.

Mitch glanced around the room, assessing it. It was comfortably appointed with a king-sized bed that was possible for him and Dani to share without making contact. The table and chairs on one side of the room would give them somewhere to work and the door and windows to the courtyard provided a clear view of anyone coming and going. Possibly problematic, although it did afford a way for a fast exit as well.

As he met Dani's gaze, he noted her inquisitive look and said, "Mr. Lazlo, I'm going to put you on speaker so Dani can hear you."

With that, he hit a button and laid the modified PDA on the tabletop.

"Good morning, Dani. I trust you liked the little gift I sent."

"Luscious, Uncle Corbett. I assume the DVDs and disk contain some information you would like us to review?" Dani reached in and took out the slim jewel cases, shuffling through them to examine their labels.

"Cordez had her staff gather some additional information for you. There are surveillance videos of the areas where the agents were killed. Their backgrounds and other information about what they were working on. The hard drive contains their case files, along with full reports on Randy Kruger. His past activities and connections," Lazlo said, and Mitch met Dani's questioning gaze.

"That's a lot of information to review before we see—"

Lazlo cut him off. "We would have provided this to you in Paris, but I had been advised by my SIS contact that Kruger would immediately be available and time wouldn't allow it."

"And now?" Dani asked as she removed the portable hard drive from the basket, set it next to the DVDs and then rearranged the fruit in the basket.

An uneasy cough came from Lazlo before he said, "It appears it will take at least another day to make Kruger available. There's interference from someone higher up at SIS. Possibly one of the deputy directors."

"Do you know who's causing the problem?" Dani asked and moved the basket to one side of the table so they would have a clear area for setting up their equipment.

"No, I don't, but I suspect the reasons are more personal than professional. I didn't keep many friends after my stint at SIS," Lazlo said.

Mitch braced one hand against the table as he asked, "So it may not be possible—"

"It will. Much as some of my old friends might not like it, I will get access to Kruger. It may take longer, but I trust you two have enough to keep you occupied until then."

Mitch glanced down at the DVDs and disk, but then his gaze swept to the bed and back, as did Dani's. When she finally looked up at him, worry had crept into her features. He sought to dispel it. "We're professionals, Corbett. We know what we need to do."

"Good, lad. You have access to our headquarters in Rome

if you need anything else. As soon as Kruger is available, I will be in touch."

The click over the PDA speaker was followed by dead air.

Mitch slipped the PDA back onto his belt and glanced at Dani.

"So, what do you want to do first?" she asked.

He walked to the door and removed the Do Not Disturb sign from the knob. With a grin, he slipped the sign on the exterior knob, then closed the door and faced her.

"We do what's expected of any newlyweds, right?"

Chapter 5

Dani's gaze skittered from Mitch to the bed and back to Mitch again. Then she understood he was just kidding. For a moment she had thought he might be serious.

Seemingly well aware that he'd pushed her buttons, he shot her a knowing grin. He walked over and motioned to the table. "Want to set up the equipment here?"

"It's as good a place as any." She whirled from him quickly, wanting to hide the flush of color heating her cheeks. Grabbing her bag, she tossed it on the bed and immediately unpacked, removing her drab-colored clothes, short black wig and toiletries and efficiently stowing them away so she could get to the laptop and other equipment she had secured beneath the soft goods.

Mitch did the same. As she'd suspected, his bag held a greater assortment of clothing, so by the time she had her equipment assembled on the table, he had only just reached the section in his bag that held his computer and the supplies they had agreed to bring with them.

She held up the DVDs. "I guess I'll get started with these until you're ready."

"I won't be long. I want to put in some surveillance cameras so we can make sure the room stays secure."

She nodded and slipped the first DVD into her laptop. It contained information on the murder of the Lazlo agent in Prague. The intelligence consisted of video from the various cameras near the Lazlo Prague offices as well as detailed reports on the investigations into his death. Also on the DVD were copies of all the open files on the cases the operative had been working at the time of his death.

Not wanting to let the reports influence her and possibly lead her to wrong first impressions about the video feeds, she left them for last. As she opened the initial MPEG file, she watched out of the corner of her eye as Mitch worked on slipping a needle-fine fiber-optic camera into a picture frame on the opposite side of the room.

He pulled the PDA from his belt and fiddled with something before he walked to another section of the room and went to work again.

Deciding he had things under control, she started playing the video—footage of the front of an ordinary-looking building, apparently the Lazlo location in Prague. Few pedestrians passed in front, and not much more motor vehicle traffic moved by the site. Either the area was not that well-frequented or it was early in the morning.

She decided morning had made the difference in the traffic conditions since it seemed slightly dark at first, but within a short period of time, the sun rose behind the building. A small alley a few doors down from the building was in shadow thanks to its western-facing opening and the larger structures around it. A good hiding place for an early-morning capture or kill.

Advancing through the video, she noted an occasional car or pedestrian, but not much activity until a well-dressed man walked north toward the Lazlo offices. He looked downward, his attention totally focused on the morning newspaper in one hand. He held a briefcase in the other.

As he passed the alley she had noted earlier, someone grabbed him.

The video lacked sound so it was impossible to tell what was happening in the shadows of the alley. Besides, the killer had probably had a silencer on his weapon.

"Find something?" Mitch asked as he finally sat at his computer, right beside her.

"The agent's capture and, presumably, where he was killed." She gestured to her screen and replayed the segment. "He never realized what hit him."

Mitch detected the mix of condemnation and distress in Dani's voice. He opted to focus on the first. "He wasn't really a secret-agent type. More like a bean counter. His latest assignment was to investigate the financial records of a charitable foundation. Maybe he was murdered to stop him from discovering a connection between the foundation and SNAKE."

"So he probably had no idea he had been targeted or how to handle it."

Mitch nodded. "Once you get to the report, it will probably indicate that there was little sign of a struggle."

Dani faced him. "And the rest of the dead operatives? Also non-secret-agent types?"

He winced and rubbed at the scar down the middle of his abdomen. "Not really. The agents killed were a mix, but I'm told they all had one thing in common—each of their cases could possibly be connected to the crime syndicate."

Dani's gaze tracked the motion of his hand, but then she ripped it away and back to the screen. "I'd like to make that call for myself after I get a chance to review all this material. It's also possible there's no connection between them and SNAKE."

"Then what's the reason for targeting them?"

"Do sadistic killers need a reason? Besides, I get the sense Lazlo may have made a few enemies over the years," she said and focused her attention solely on the video.

She had shut him out. Fine by him, Mitch thought and turned to the copies of the case files on the hard drive. He first downloaded them to his computer and then shut down the portable drive, disconnected it and passed it to Dani.

"Thanks," she murmured without taking her eyes from her screen, where she reviewed digitally enhanced sections of what video they had. Whoever had done the kills had been very good, leaving few clues for them to follow.

His examination of the case files confirmed there was little information except the killer's unique MO on the last two kills. The first two attacks…

He once again rubbed his scar, recalling how Kruger had surprised him on one of the narrow side streets not far from their current location. He had been distracted, worried about how Kruger had managed to elude them. He had also been concerned about what might happen if the chase left the narrow, twisting side streets and exploded out onto the more crowded neighborhood avenues. Kruger would have not been above opening fire even with innocents nearby—collateral damage meant nothing to people like him. Dani was right that sadistic killers didn't care.

Or people like Dani, he thought, shooting a glance at her

and wondering whether when she was on duty as the Sparrow she had cared about those around her. About him, he thought, his mind drifting back to the day he had "died."

An arm snaked around his neck and Mitch instinctively knew what would follow.

Reaching upward, he managed to block the swipe of the knife at his throat, but the blade bit deep, slicing across his forearm.

He ignored the pain and dipped his shoulder, used the shift in his weight to throw his attacker up and over him.

Kruger landed with a thud, but before Mitch could attack, his legs started to buckle. He wondered about it for a second, but then looked down and noticed the handle of the knife buried deep in his midsection.

Staggering back, he shifted to remove the blade, only Kruger swiftly jumped to his feet. He lunged at Mitch, grabbed the knife and drove upward with it, a vicious smile on his face.

As he struggled to stay upright, Mitch hit the wall behind him, which kept him on his feet for only a second as his legs finally gave out and he slumped to the ground.

Kruger bent toward him then, intent on finishing the job.

He tried to raise the hand that still held his gun, but his body refused to cooperate. Kruger didn't have to worry about him. It would only be a short amount of time before he was dead. He could tell from the way all the warmth in his body pooled at his center, trying to keep his vital organs functioning. It was a futile effort. He sensed the growing trail of heat down the middle of his body from the blood escaping him.

Kruger stopped suddenly and shot a quick glance up the

side street. With a look of fear etched on his face, he bolted away and out into one of the bigger thoroughfares.

He had to let Aidan know what was happening, Mitch thought, fumbling for the cell phone at his belt—only, his fingers seemed inflexible. Thick and useless.

A moment later, a shadow passed before his eyes and suddenly Dani appeared, kneeling beside him.

"Oh god, Mitch. God, no," she said, slipping an arm around his upper body and cradling him close.

"Dani…be…safe," he somehow managed to say and found the strength to pick up the hand holding the gun. He placed it over hers, where it rested at his midsection, trying to stem the flow of blood. He pressed the gun into her hand.

"Take it. Stay safe…love you." The words were interspersed with his rough, pain-filled breaths.

Dani stroked his cheek, wet with her tears. "Hold on, love. I'm going to get help."

"No…time. Be…careful," he warned her, worried that Kruger would come back to rid himself of Dani as well. He suspected she had likely witnessed all or part of the attack. Kruger would want to leave no witnesses behind.

Dani bent her head, dropped a kiss on his forehead and then another on his lips. "I love you, Mitch. Please, just stay with me a little longer. I'm calling for help."

A second later, she instructed over her cell phone. "This is Sparrow. I need medical assistance…"

"Mitch?"

He seemed surprised when Dani repeated his name. "Are you okay?"

"When did you find out Kruger's location?" he asked, apparently shaking off whatever had been troubling him.

The question came out of left field and threw her. "What? Why are you asking—"

"SNAKE. It's got to be them behind this. I think that we'll eventually find all the dots connect these attacks to them."

Dani shrugged. "It may seem that way—"

"May *seem* that way?" Mitch challenged and shot up off his chair. He paced back and forth before facing her and raking a hand through his hair in frustration. "What kind of proof do you need?"

Proof? She had it every time she looked into a mirror, and so did Mitch. They both bore the scars from the crime organization's attacks, but the other deaths might be just sheer coincidence.

"Why single out the Lazlo Group? Unless it was because you were all getting too close to SNAKE's operations, only…"

"Only what?" he challenged.

"These kills. The latest MO indicates there's more to it. These are personal. A challenge. But how can we determine the motive when we don't know who really runs the syndicate these days now that Max Dumont is dead?"

"So the Sparrow didn't even come close to completing her mission?" He placed his hands on his hips and glared at her, egging her on.

Dani refused to take the bait. She rose from her chair and walked to stand before him. Looking up at his greater height, she said, "I didn't complete my mission because I let my personal feelings get in the way. I'm not going to do that again, Mitch, so you can stop goading me."

His shoulders slumped and he released a tired sigh. "I'm sorry. It's just that—"

"You need defenses. I understand. I need them, too."

She shocked him with her confession almost as much as

she surprised herself. She hadn't meant to admit that she needed to protect herself from the feelings she still had for him. But maybe it was better that it was all out in the open. That both of them were aware of it so as to avoid problems.

When he didn't say anything else, she said, "It's time for a break. I need some air."

"Then let's roll," he said and suddenly became all-action guy. He shut down his computer, packed it and the portable hard drive into a small bag that he tossed over his shoulder.

Following his lead, she stowed the DVDs and her laptop in a stylish leather knapsack—her one concession to fashion—and made sure that when she slipped it on she still had easy access to the Glock in the holster at the small of her back.

She watched as Mitch checked the same, but then he slipped another PDA from his bag and walked to the table, which was now devoid of any telltale items. Only the fruit basket and typical hotel paraphernalia rested there.

Mitch slipped the second PDA under the table and pressed upward, apparently adhering it to the underside. "This will broadcast the video signals via a satellite connection to one of the Lazlo servers. We'll be able to access the recorded videos or live feeds from our PDAs or any PC. That way we'll know if the area's been compromised."

"Sounds good. What about the exterior sector?"

"We should stay out until dark. It'll be easier to plant the cameras then."

"So we familiarize ourselves with the area—"

"And grab dinner. I'm hungry," he said.

She smiled, plucked a pear from the basket and tossed it to him. "It's too early to eat dinner in Rome. This should tide you over for a few hours."

He caught the pear and grinned. "You're a hard taskmaster, Sparrow."

"I'm glad you figured that out, Agent Lama. Makes life easier for both of us."

The grin on his face slowly faded and he took a step closer, reached up and cupped her cheek, the action achingly familiar.

In low bedroom tones, he said, "I suspect life with you could never be easy."

She inched her chin up defiantly. "Are you so sure about that, or are you too afraid to find out?"

Chapter 6

Dani didn't wait for his reply, afraid of what it might be. She charged out of the room, and Mitch quickly followed, catching up to her to stroll side-by-side into the courtyard. As Dani noticed the hotel clerk by one set of doors, tending to a large terra-cotta pot filled with flowers, she stepped closer to Mitch and wrapped an arm around his waist.

Mitch eased an arm around her, pulling her tight against him. He bent his head, nuzzled the side of her cheek and whispered, "You'll have to make this look good, you know."

She went up on tiptoe and silenced him with a kiss, pressing her body to his, opening her mouth to taste him and run her tongue along the outline of his lips. When he groaned, she shifted away slightly and whispered in his ear, "Was that good enough, *amore?*"

"Too good," he muttered beneath his breath and shifted inches away, a bright flush of color on his cheeks. He waved

at the clerk but applied gentle pressure at the small of her back
to urge her in the opposite direction and out of the courtyard.

They remained close together, arms around each other's
waists until they reached a larger street a few blocks away.
Dani separated from him then and stopped to get her bearings.
It had been over a year since she had been in Rome, but it took
her only a second to know where she was.

"Lazlo offices are across the river. Actually, quite a
distance away. There's a tram we could take."

Mitch glanced up the street, scoping it out before facing
her. "Are you up to hoofing it?"

"Hoofing it? If you're up to it, then so am I." Besides, she
could use the exercise and time to stretch. The annoying pull
she had experienced along her midsection the other day had
come back with a vengeance, likely from sitting so many
hours as she watched the videos.

At his nod, she started walking, intent on reaching the
Tiber. Mitch matched his longer strides to her shorter ones.
She kept the pace steady but reasonable. It was quite a walk
to the Lazlo Group location, which was on a small street
close to the Spanish Steps and the Villa Borghese.

It was odd walking beside him in uneasy silence, considering how many times they had been together in Rome. In that
wonderful year, whenever had Mitch visited, they had regularly strolled the streets, exploring the sights of the ancient
city. The talk had been non stop then, as had been the loving.

Of course, none of that was possible any longer. He had
deceived her—as she had him. The fact that both of their deceptions had been for good cause did nothing to alleviate the concern
that they both had carried out their deceptions quite well.

It left her wary, uncertain of whether Mitch's actions

could be trusted now, and yet his honor had been one of the things that had drawn her to him in the first place. As for her own deception...

It had been necessary in her quest for justice.

At the river, she gestured toward one of the bridges, but as they crossed over the small square cobblestones, she paused to look over the sluggishly moving waters to the other bridges down river—the Ponte Garibaldi and, just beyond it, the small Isola Tiberina in the midst of the Tiber.

"Something wrong?" Mitch asked.

She laid her hands on his. "Loosen up, Mitch. Just pausing to enjoy the view."

Mitch glanced over his shoulder, tracking Dani's gaze. The river and bridges stretched out before him, a nice view, much as she had said. But not as nice as the view in front of him.

He faced her once again, telling himself he shouldn't take such pleasure in seeing her. In walking with her along these streets as they had three years earlier. But the pleasure was as undeniable as the pain that followed at the realization of all they had lost. Somehow, the last didn't communicate itself to his brain as he said, "Yes, nice view."

Bright color blossomed along her cheeks as she apparently realized his attention was on her. "Let's go. It's starting to get dark."

Dusk approached quickly, a testament to how many hours they had spent reviewing the materials Lazlo had sent. His stomach growled, a reminder that the boy from Baltimore hadn't ever gotten accustomed to late-night European meals.

Dani grinned at the rather loud noise from his midsection. With a playful tug on his hand, she said, "Come on. It'll be tough to sneak up on anyone with all that grumbling going on."

Her pace was faster than before and they were soon at a familiar place, the Campo de Fiori. He remembered shopping away many a morning with her among the assorted vendors' stalls. At this hour they were gone, clearing the plaza for artist types and the outdoor dining spots that the restaurants along the edges of the piazza set up.

"Just a snack, mind you," Dani warned as she pulled him along to a tiny café. In perfect Italian she ordered some cappuccinos and buttered rolls.

He'd had something more substantial in mind, but this would tide him over for another couple of hours. He sipped slowly at the cappuccino in between bites of the deliciously yeasty and buttery roll. He was done long before Dani, who shot him a look out of the corner of her eye and took pity on him, handing him her half-eaten roll.

"But keep your hands off the coffee," she warned him.

He chuckled, earning a dimpled grin from her. He reminded himself to keep this all business between them. It was about the mission and nothing else.

He reined in his reactions to her—those of his heart and body—and sipped the coffee and ate the roll that suddenly wasn't as tasty. He was too busy recalling the taste of Dani's mouth and lips against his.

They finished quickly and continued on their way. The walk took them past the Pantheon and through an assortment of small streets to the Via dei Corso. He remembered that the Trevi fountain stood just a stone's throw away, and he took the lead, but when they reached it, the area was mobbed as always by tourists. The way it had been the first time Dani had brought him there.

They had waited then, inching their way to the edge of the fountain where Dani had playfully slipped a handful of coins into his hand and he had turned and tossed them over his shoulder to ensure his return to Rome as legend claimed.

And he had returned, time and time again, to see her. Each visit filled with pleasure until the realization had come that he was in love with her. But she hadn't been the woman he had thought, he reminded himself. He didn't know if he could get over that or deal with her quest for vengeance for her parents' deaths. The file Lazlo had given him on Dani said that she hadn't gotten that information from Donovan. That quest had consumed her before, and he was certain he could never replace it as her number one priority.

He put his head down, ignoring the fountain, and pushed onward until they reached the Via Condotti, where they passed an assortment of elegant shops as they approached the Spanish Steps.

Beside him, Dani paused and gestured to something that looked like little more than an alley.

"This way," she said and slipped into the narrow street.

He followed, trusting that she knew her way better than he did. Sure enough, within a few minutes the alley opened into another street lined with shops and supply houses that likely provided the materials for the larger fashion houses on the Via Condotti and closer to the Spanish Steps.

At one corner, a quick motion of Dani's head identified the building to him. On the exterior it appeared to be a store selling fashion trimmings. Its front window displayed an assortment of buttons, ribbons and embellishments, but he knew that a couple of stories below the shop was the location of the Lazlo Group's Rome headquarters.

They paused for a moment, reconnoitering the area. Scoping out the access to the building. Making mental note of everything nearby, because they knew they had to be prepared for anything and everything. They both understood that possibly better than any others.

As Dani mimicked examining some fabrics in the window of a store across the street from the Lazlo offices, Mitch leaned against the stone column beside the window. He noted the vehicular traffic going by as well as the pedestrians, mostly shoppers with bags from the larger stores on Via Condotti.

Beside him, Dani muttered what sounded like a curse beneath her breath and rubbed at her side, snagging his attention. She looked pale. Or maybe it just seemed that way thanks to all the black she wore, from her sneakers to her jeans and shirt.

"You okay?" He straightened and laid a hand on her shoulder.

"Just a stitch," she said, but it was obvious that it was more. He wondered if he had misjudged her physical readiness for the mission and was about to question her comment, but knew Dani wouldn't take kindly to coddling.

"Good. I mean...good that it's only a stitch." *You're an ass,* he thought and then his stomach growled more loudly than before, dragging a chuckle out of Dani, who seemed to leap on the opportunity it presented.

"Do you think you can hold out until we get back to Trastevere?"

"Are you up to walking back?" He winced as she immediately got her guard up.

"I can make it. Can you?" She lifted her chin in challenge.

Discretion, he told himself. "Actually, no. I'm tired and hungry and I'd like to get back to the room because we don't want to disappoint Signora Garibaldi."

She grinned at the mention of the exuberant hotel clerk who had checked them in earlier that day. "I guess we need to give her something to talk about."

"Definitely need to keep up our cover, so let's hit the bricks." He slipped his arm around her waist and that she didn't protest was maybe a sign that she wasn't feeling a hundred percent.

"Hit the bricks? Do you realize—"

"How clichéd I can be? Yep. Did you forget that about me?"

Dani wanted to say that she hadn't forgotten anything about him, but bit back that comment since it would only cause trouble. She hadn't forgotten his propensity for such sayings or the way it felt when he tucked her under his arm protectively, as he had now. She might have protested, if she was feeling better, but the stitch in her side hadn't receded. If anything, it had grown worse with the long walk.

She told herself that what she needed was rest and then a nice stretching session. Possibly a long soak in the bath.

"We can catch a tram back not far from here." She motioned in the direction of Via Condotti and they walked side-by-side a few blocks until they were at the tram stop. It wasn't long before the tram came, but it was relatively crowded, forcing them to stand close together.

Dani relaxed against Mitch's solid bulk, letting him battle the bumps and jostling of the crowd, and wondered when she had become such a baby. She had chased after bad guys with broken bones, and now she was letting a little discomfort in her side get to her.

Maybe it's because now you know what it feels like to die, her inner voice reminded her. And so she allowed herself the protection of Mitch's body and the support of his arms. By the time the tram had crossed over the Tiber and into Trastevere, the sharp pain in her side had receded to a dull throb.

Mitch leaned down and whispered in her ear. "When should we get off?"

"One more stop, I think. By Santa Cecilia," she replied. Realizing they were almost there, she took hold of his hand and urged him to the exit.

She didn't release her hold once they were off the tram. Instead she guided him down one of the nearby streets, Via de Genovesi, and to the restaurant.

Spirito di Vino was well-known for its food, wine and having Rome's original synagogue in its cellar. They walked up the stone steps, beneath an archway and into the restaurant. Once inside, she noted that the stone Alcantara walls continued within along with the archways. Since they were still a bit early for the late-eating Italians, the wait for a table was blessedly short.

The friendly hostess seated them and presented the menus, but also advised that if they desired, the staff would be glad to offer their recommendations for the meal along with the wine.

Mitch, who was sitting beside her, laid his hand over hers. For the first time, the glint of the gold wedding band on his ring finger registered. Reminded her of the similar ring she wore on her hand as part of their charade. How many times had she imagined them married for real? More times than she cared to admit.

"Does that sound good to you, honey?" It was his newlywed husband voice, all solicitous and eager.

"Of course, sweetheart. This is our honeymoon and we want it to be special."

At her words, the hostess smiled. "*Benissimo*. We will make sure that it will be *molto especiale per lei*."

"*Grazie, signora*," Mitch said with a polite nod.

When the hostess walked away, she leaned forward and said, "So you speak a little Italian?"

"Just enough to say, 'thank you', 'please' and 'where's the

bathroom.' Not fluent like you. Did you learn it while on assignment here?"

She shrugged. "It was one of my minors in college."

"The University of Silvershire?" Hidden behind his words lurked another question—one that asked, "How much of what you told me about yourself was true?"

A waiter came over and poured two glasses of pinot grigio for them. She picked up the glass and said, "To our honeymoon."

He clicked his glass with hers and took a sip, as she did. The wine was fruity and refreshing.

The waiter immediately returned with a plate of *formaggio mixto*—various cheeses—and a basket filled with an assortment of artisanal bread and rolls.

It was a nice way to begin the meal, she thought, and ate a bit of gorgonzola and semolina bread before answering Mitch.

"I got my degree there. I majored in political science with minors in Italian and French."

"Any other languages I should know about?"

"German and Russian. I had started on Arabic when…"

Mitch picked up on Dani's disquiet as her voice trailed off. When he met her gaze, he realized that she had stopped when he had left her life.

"Why?" he asked.

Her small-boned shoulders barely shifted with her shrug. "It just didn't seem important anymore. All that knowledge and skills when I'd…when I'd lost another person I loved."

His gut twisted at her words, alternately pleased and sad at her confession. He chose to shift the conversation to another place. "What happened with the prince, with Reginald—"

"Wasn't something I intended to happen," she immediately defended.

He thought about the prince's death from the tainted cocaine Dani had left behind. She hadn't outright killed him. And yet… "But you were there when he took the cocaine. You were then when he died."

The hand bringing a piece of cheese and bread to her mouth trembled for a moment. She completed the action, chewed slowly, thoughtfully, before she answered him.

"Reginald swore he was clean. I left the room for only a few minutes…and when I returned he was dead from the cocaine. He'd lied to me about his drug use."

"But did he deserve to die for that?" Mitch grabbed a piece of cheese from the plate and popped it into his mouth. The flavor was sharp and strong, much like Dani's response.

"People like Reginald never stop to consider how many people die so they can get high. All I wanted was justice."

"There's a difference between justice and vengeance, isn't there?"

Dani's eyes narrowed as she considered him. "Why do you care?"

Why did he? he asked himself. He'd promised to not make it personal between them, but a part of him wanted to know that the woman he had loved wasn't a cold-blooded murderer. "Because I do care, Dani. I want to know why punishing Reginald was so important. Why you wrecked your career at SIS. Why you risked it all."

She leaned forward, never shifting her gaze from his. "Because Donovan promised me the names of the drug dealers who had killed my parents. I wanted them punished. I wanted to find out who headed the crime syndicate they worked for, because I didn't want another family to suffer as mine did."

Mitch placed his hand over hers again. Her fingers were chilled, and he twined them with his. "I understand, Dani. I may not approve—"

She ripped her hand from his. "I didn't ask for your approval, Mitch. Or your understanding."

No, she hadn't, but he sensed that she needed both from him. That *he* needed to know and understand. He wanted Dani to be a hero again. He had thought of her that way when Lazlo had explained that Dani worked for SIS. That she was a good guy. Some part of him recognized that, while imperfect, she still was.

The meal passed quickly but silently after that. It made for a quick dinner, which was fine since they still had a lot of material to review while they waited for Lazlo to arrange for them to see Kruger.

Then it would be time to get some sleep.

In the king-sized bed.

Next to Dani.

As he watched her devour the last of the panna cotta and the half of the cannoli he had offered her, he recalled that sweets weren't her only weakness—she'd had a soft spot for sex with him.

As they rose from the table, their gazes met. Hers was wary, as if she didn't know what he thought about her earlier confession regarding her role in the prince's death and the why of it.

He wanted to set the record straight. Needed to let her know how he felt.

"I won't judge you for what you did."

"But can you forgive me for it?" she asked, wrapping her arms around herself.

He sensed the forgiveness she sought had to do with more

than just the prince, but he wasn't sure he could forgive all that had happened between them.

"Maybe," he said, and the tension left her body with that one small word.

It was a start.

Chapter 7

The walk back to the hotel was short. Luckily, the courtyard sat empty when they entered, giving him the perfect opportunity to plant the surveillance equipment.

As they approached the door to their room, Mitch scoped out possible locations for the cameras and noticed the terracotta planter attached to the wall by their door. Perfect, he thought, and when they reached their room, he applied subtle pressure to Dani's waist.

She looked up at him, and he inclined his head in the direction of the planter.

With a nod, she turned and leaned against the small section of wall between the door and the flowers. Shooting him a come-hither look, she wrapped an arm around his waist and pulled him close as if for a kiss. She whispered against his lips, "Where are the cameras?"

"My left jeans pocket," he murmured before kissing her. She slipped her fingers into his pocket and removed the cameras.

Unfortunately, the feel of her fingers there sent his body into immediate overdrive, and he knew Dani couldn't fail to notice.

"Mitch?" she asked as he shifted away, allowing her to transfer the cameras to her other hand. She picked up that hand, ran it up the arm he had braced against the wall by the planter. As she slipped him one camera, he bent his head and kissed her again, wanting to maintain their cover.

Wanting to kiss her.

He fumbled with slipping the camera into a secure spot among the flowers. He felt the brush of her empty hand as it trailed back down his arm, confirming that she had secured hers.

Only she didn't pull her hand away, leaving it to linger at his shoulder. She opened her mouth as he deepened the kiss until they were both straining against one another, bodies pressed tightly together as passion overwhelmed common sense.

The scuff of a footstep had them hastily breaking apart.

It was one of the staff, making a delivery. The young woman carried a tray to a door several rooms away.

Mitch looked at Dani, who opened the door to their room, quickly entered and once there, ignored him, immediately moving to the table, where she placed her bag and began setting up her equipment.

Which was as it should be, Mitch thought. The kiss at the door had lingered long after their job had been finished. It could only be classified as a major mistake no matter how good it had felt.

And tasted. Sweet like the panna cotta and cannoli cream from the restaurant.

He ruthlessly drove that thought away and copied Dani's

actions, mechanically removing his laptop and the portable disk drive. Slowly taking a place beside her as he resisted the urge to continue the kissing fest with her.

"Is everything fine?" she asked.

"Fine," he grunted, easing the PDA back onto his belt and powering up his laptop.

A lot of work needed to be done by the morning, and it was time to get to it. He told himself not to be annoyed that Dani seemed unaffected by their little interlude and forced himself to work.

By late the next morning, she and Mitch had a list of everyone connected to Mitch's attack and the three subsequent killings as well as all those involved with her mission to catch Kruger.

Except for the obvious connections relating to Kruger, not one name had been repeated on any of their lists. Which meant that they had to move out a degree of connection. Maybe the link was someone her handler had spoken with or someone at Lazlo whom Mitch and his former partner Aidan had contacted, although it seemed as if Corbett Lazlo himself kept direct contact with most of his agents on high-profile cases.

The pain in her side had subsided to a dull bearable ache the night before, but sitting for hours this morning had reignited the fire along her midsection. While Mitch began extending his search to the next level, she rose and stepped to the center of the room. Stretching her arms above her, she immediately regretted the action as it created an even sharper jabbing pain.

"You okay?" Mitch turned her way, and she realized she must have made some noise to signal her discomfort.

"Just a cramp," she replied lamely. Mitch didn't buy it for a second, but didn't press or attempt to solicit a different response from her. He seemed to have hardened himself to her last night after that kiss at the door and in a way, she was thankful for it. The kiss…well, the kiss had turned into more than either of them wanted.

Even the simple act of reaching into his jeans pocket had produced complications. Her hand had itched to slip lower, cover the erection that had suddenly come to life and pressed against the flatness of her belly.

Lying in the bed beside him last night had been sheer torture as she'd imagined what might happen if they somehow both shifted from clinging to the edges of the bed and moved into the big, comfortable center of it.

Mitch's cell phone sounded loudly, pulling her from the distracting thoughts.

"Lama here." His curt, military-precise tone spoke of his service as an Army Ranger.

"Yes, Corbett. Dani and I have been at work on the materials you sent."

Mitch waved for her to come over and turned on the speaker. As she approached the table he said, "No connections so far. We're broadening our search."

"Maybe speaking with Kruger will yield some results. He's been transferred from an SIS holding facility in London to the care of another Lazlo operative, who is transporting him to the Rome location. We expect him to arrive at headquarters within an hour or so."

"We'll be there," Dani said and shot a look at Mitch, who agreed with a bob of his head.

"Good. I trust the two of you to know what to do."

With that, Lazlo signed off, leaving her and Mitch to accomplish their task—finding out which of the people Kruger had spoken with had possibly blown her cover.

Kruger might have crapped his pants if the Sparrow had walked into the small room where he was being held. Their last encounter had left them both rather bloody.

Kruger had put up a hell of fight when she had finally cornered him, and she had been only too happy to oblige, needing to exact punishment for his killing Mitch. It had taken weeks for the bruises from the encounter to go away.

She only hoped Kruger had suffered a little longer. The dossier Lazlo had provided hadn't offered much information other than the names of the operatives who had interrogated Kruger after his capture, the schedule Kruger was allowed at the holding facility and the name of the attorney trying to get him a hearing.

The last bit of information had surprised her. Barrett Jenkins was one of London's more well-known solicitors, with connections to some of the country's most influential leaders, including a man who some said might be Britain's next prime minister, John Breckenridge.

That Jenkins represented scum like Kruger troubled her and Mitch alike after she pointed it out to him. Especially considering that the Lazlo Group believed someone highly placed in either SIS or the government might be responsible for the leaks that had nearly cost both her and Mitch their lives.

As much as Dani wanted to see shock and fear enter Kruger's eyes if the Sparrow were to reappear, it was too soon for her alter-ego to rise from the dead.

She tucked the last of her hair under the short black wig she had brought with her and watched as Mitch slipped on a shoulder-length brown wig. He had eschewed his normal casual style, namely a conservative polo and khakis, for faded and ripped jeans and a tight T-shirt that showed off every muscle and the tribal tattoo. Combined with the long hair and the dark stubble he hadn't shaved off that morning, he looked decidedly dangerous.

And not just in an I-can-kick-your-ass kind of way.

Aware that her drab clothes might possibly give her away as the Sparrow, she had opted to slip out of their hotel room shortly after Lazlo's call to purchase several outfits at a local vintage store. She now looked like a throwback to the sixties in a brightly colored tie-dyed tank top and black miniskirt that showed off a lot of leg above the black knee-high boots she had also found at the store.

Shooting a last look at Mitch and then at Kruger through the one-way mirror in the interrogation room, she asked, "Ready?"

Mitch was ready, but not to interrogate Kruger, he thought, appreciating the sight of Dani's nicely shaped legs and derriere, not to mention the way the tank top showed off her small waist and perfect breasts.

He suspected Kruger would likely be appreciating the same things, which might make the questioning a little easier. While he didn't want to denigrate his own kind, he had to acknowledge that men generally had a tendency to act stupid around gorgeous women, and Dani was just that.

Gorgeous.

"Ready," he replied and had to wipe his suddenly sweaty hands along the soft fabric of the jeans. He only hoped Dani wouldn't notice what else was happening beneath the denim.

She whirled on one high heel and walked out of the room, seemingly oblivious to his physical state, the skirt giving an inviting little bounce against her back side. He followed her, barely containing a groan.

Down boy, he reminded himself. He had to focus on facing the man who had nearly killed him three years earlier.

With a deep breath, he walked in behind Dani.

Dani felt Mitch's gaze on her as they entered the room. Showtime. Kruger slouched in a chair, seeming rather bored by it all, but as Mitch and Dani entered, he popped up. Their captive gave Dani a rather intense perusal, his eyes roving rapaciously over her curves.

"My, my. What have we here?" Kruger began and tracked her passage around the back of his chair. She took a spot beside him and leaned her butt on the edge of the table directly next to Kruger, who continued with, "Cute little birdie and…"

He paused and looked at Mitch, who took a spot in front of the table. "Are you the muscle, mate?"

With a quick glance at Mitch, Dani said, "We have some questions for you, Mr. Kruger."

Kruger leaned close and sniffed. "You don't smell like SIS. CIA, maybe?"

"What we are, are two people who can make your life rather unpleasant if you're not cooperative," Mitch replied as Dani inched closer to Kruger and laid a hand on his shoulder.

The man tracked his gaze up Dani's arm to her breasts, where they lingered before he moved upward to meet her gaze. "Sorry, birdie, but my lawyer—"

"Barrett Jenkins. Rather high-priced talent for scum like you," Dani said.

Kruger shrugged, trying to act nonchalant, but beneath Dani's hand, the tension of his muscles communicated itself to her. "Guess someone else is footing the bill. Who might that be?" she asked.

Their captive shifted his gaze away to Mitch, shrugged

again before replying, "I'm a dead man, remember? No one knows I exist anymore."

"Someone is paying Jenkins's fees. Who is it, Mr. Kruger?" she repeated.

"Like I said, birdie, I'm a nobody whose civil rights are being violated. Mr. Jenkins understands that."

She smiled and slid back a little. Picking up one booted foot, she placed it on his thigh, giving him an eyeful of lean leg, which the slimeball was quick to take advantage of.

He raised his hand and eased it over her thigh, stroked it. With a quick toss of his head in Mitch's direction, he said, "Lose the muscle and I could definitely find some answers for you."

She sensed Mitch's motion toward the table from behind her and it proved enough of a distraction to Kruger. While he looked toward Mitch, she snared his hand and quickly had him in a painful hold, his thumb bent back.

Kruger flinched and tried to rip his hand away, but she had it secured too tightly. To add to her control, she shifted the leg on his thigh to his crotch and applied the barest amount of pressure with her booted foot.

It was enough to quiet their prisoner.

"Some men like it painful, Mr. Kruger. Do you?" she said, leaning forward until she was almost nose to nose with him.

"You're not playing nice, luv."

She increased the pressure on his thumb, pulling a wince from him. "Who hired Jenkins?"

"Don't know," he said, and Mitch seized on that answer to come around the far side of the table.

He approached and took a position on the other side of Kruger, sitting on the table much like Dani was, with his arms folded across his chest, emphasizing the deep, thick muscles of his physique.

For one millisecond, Dani allowed herself to imagine those arms wrapped around her, but then she returned to the questioning. "If you think this is painful, imagine what it will be like when my friend takes over."

Their prisoner's gaze swept back and forth between the two of them. He gulped, his Adam's apple visibly bobbing in his scrawny neck with his discomfort. "I don't know jack about why Jenkins is suddenly my new best friend."

She met Mitch's gaze for a second and immediately understood a change was in order.

"Tell us about the operative you knifed three years ago. Who warned you he would be there?" she said, easing the pressure of her foot against his crotch, but only a little.

"The Sparrow was the one who put the knife in his gut, not me."

She increased the pressure on his thumb and warned, "Your jewels are next if you don't start telling the truth."

"It *is* the truth."

"I watched the Sparrow die, mate," Mitch said, leaning close to the other man and mimicking his accent. "She spilled her guts to me as her blood spilled over my hands. She didn't do it."

Once again, Dani felt the tension in Kruger's body and for a painful moment, realized that in one way, Mitch had gone through the Sparrow's death, since the woman she had been before had perished.

Adopting the good-cop posture, she shifted to whisper in their prisoner's ear, "You don't want to get him angry, Randy. All you need to do is provide some information."

"I was transporting some merchandise for a client."

"*Merchandise* being another word for illegal-conflict diamonds?" she said as she settled back onto the table and released his thumb.

"I didn't know what I was carrying until one day the bag broke."

"Is that why someone wanted you dead? Because you discovered what was in the shipments you were carrying?" Mitch asked, although they were both aware that some of Kruger's shipments had turned up short, apparently angering the intended recipients. It was why the Sparrow had been hired by SNAKE to dispose of him.

Uneasily, Kruger's gaze flickered between her and Mitch, as if he sensed they knew the real answer. Maybe because of that, he responded truthfully. "I had my fingers in the pot. Figured no one would notice if a few diamonds went missing here and there."

"You sold those diamonds to disreputable dealers?" Mitch asked. He and Aidan had been sent to capture Kruger for just that reason—one of their clients had a competitor whom he suspected of selling contraband diamonds.

When Kruger nodded, she continued. "You knew someone was coming for you. Who tipped you off?"

"The people who hired me to run the diamonds. I got a text message warning me that two operatives were nearby. Ran into one in the alley as I tried to escape."

"The operative you knifed? The one you say the Sparrow killed?" Mitch pressed, a deadly chill in his voice that transferred itself to her.

"I'd heard the rumors about how the Sparrow looked and saw someone matching the description running into the alley. I wasn't going to wait and see if it was her."

"But it *was* her. You found that out when she captured you a few days later," she reminded him, almost itching for a repeat of that capture so she could inflict some more punishment on behalf of Mitch.

"Bitch beat the crap out of me, but not before I got my licks in. I wasn't sorry to hear she's dead."

She itched to prove to him just how dead she wasn't, but held back and considered that something didn't make sense. Why would the same person who hired her to dispose of Kruger warn him about Mitch and his partner? Unless of course they wanted Kruger killed and not alive in the hands of the Lazlo Group.

"You know your employers wanted you dead. That's why they sent the Sparrow. So why are you protecting them?" she said.

"I'm just protecting myself, birdie." Kruger shifted back in his chair and crossed thin arms against his chest, a smile on his ferret-like face.

"I saw the Sparrow all teary-eyed over the operative I gutted. Heard her calling for help. Told that SIS nancy boy all about it. Thought he might want to know who his agent had been doing."

Mitch immediately jumped on that tidbit. "Who was the SIS agent you told that story to?"

Kruger quickly answered, "He didn't give me a name. He strolled in after the others had left, flashed his ID and said he had some more questions for me."

Dani pressed the issue. "Describe what he looked like."

"Why should I?" Kruger shot back, clearly growing annoyed with their questioning.

It pushed Mitch over the edge.

For a big man, he moved with frightening speed, shifting quickly behind Kruger and establishing a punishing choke hold. The smaller man grabbed at Mitch's arm, but clearly could not break free as Mitch yanked him upward. The action tipped the chair onto its two back legs, forcing Dani to remove her boot from Kruger's privates.

"Why should you?" Mitch said and jerked their captive around just a menacing bit more. "Actually, you don't have to. I'm rather enjoying this."

"Stop him," Kruger pleaded, his voice hoarse. A bluish tinge slowly developed across his features from the lack of air.

"What did he look like?" she asked, but reached out and laid a hand on Mitch's arm, silently urging him to calm down and loosen his hold.

As Mitch did so, Kruger's gaze shot back and forth between them, anxious, but finally cooperative. "Average height. Light brown hair."

With those words, Mitch relaxed his hold some more and allowed Kruger to settle back into the chair. As a parting reminder, however, he shook him once again and said, "What else?"

"Pretty, like a model. Light-colored eyes. Well-built, but not like the Incredible Hulk here." At those words, Mitch finally released the other man completely and swept back to his side of the table opposite Dani. He eased his hands across his chest and waited for her to resume the interrogation.

"Do you think you could identify this agent if we provided some pictures?" she asked.

Kruger was about to offer up yet another shrug, but with a quick look at Mitch, seemed to reconsider. Instead, he faced her and said, "Possibly. I remember him because he seemed so much younger than the rest."

"How much younger?" Mitch prompted.

"Mid-twenties. Always thought those secret-agent SIS types would be more seasoned. This pup was still wet behind the ears."

She considered that she had begun her tenure at SIS right

out of college and had assumed the role of the Sparrow not much later. Still, Kruger was right that for the greater part, the operatives sent out into the field and to interrogate prisoners—especially special ones like Kruger—had more experience and were usually older. If a newer agent were being groomed it was unlikely he'd be allowed to be alone with a prisoner.

Which meant that the mystery agent who had questioned Kruger had possibly been acting either on his own or for the benefit of someone other than SIS.

"We'll see you in the morning, Mr. Kruger," Dani said. She rose from the edge of the table and walked around to Mitch, who seemed to hesitate.

She placed her hand on his arm. Tension vibrated in the muscles there, but his outward appearance revealed nothing about his emotions. She sensed he wanted more from their prisoner. Despite that, she suspected Kruger had little more to give.

"Time to go," she told Mitch. Instead, he walked back to Kruger, laid one hand on the table and the other on the edge of Kruger's chair. Leaning close, he said to the other man, "I'm warning you now—I'm not a morning person. You'd better not do anything to piss me off. Like hold back information."

With that he pushed off and stalked to the door, where he waited for Dani to join him.

As she did so, Kruger called out, "Hey, beauty and the beast."

She turned and shot him an annoyed look, to which Kruger responded, "I just remembered something else."

Chapter 8

The something else that Kruger remembered was that the young agent had dressed sharply. The kind of sharp that came from having scads of money. With that recollection came another—the young agent had sported a gold signet ring. Kruger vaguely recollected something resembling a *T* in the fanciful letters engraved on the surface of the ring.

The ring was possibly the better lead, Mitch thought as he sat beside Dani in their room. They were both at their computers, reviewing the case files on the various SIS agents who had been officially involved with Dani's assignment as the Sparrow and with Kruger's interrogation.

None of them matched their prisoner's description of the agent. "What do you think?"

Dani stood and stretched, passing her hand over her side as she did so. A slight wince flashed across her features.

"You okay?"

"Fine," she said with a tired exhale and then continued. "Not one of these agents comes close to Kruger's description. Not to mention that the visit seems to have violated all kinds of protocols."

Mitch nodded. "Agreed. So he's a cowboy. Maybe trying to make a name for himself in the agency."

"Or maybe he's feeding the information to someone, whether it's SNAKE or a contact higher up in SIS or government circles." She stepped away from the table after she spoke and paced, continuously rubbing her side while her strides carried her back and forth across the length of the room.

"So we have three possible issues. Jenkins, this unknown mystery agent and whomever the agent is reporting to at SIS," he said.

Dani stopped and faced him. "I'm still finding it hard to believe that someone high up in SIS would jeopardize his or her career to get back at Lazlo."

"We don't know what happened when SIS tossed Lazlo out, but Lazlo came out ahead in the deal. He's rich, successful and leading an agency whose resources possibly surpass those of SIS," he said and pushed back from the table, stretched out his legs and laid his hands on his stomach.

"I guess it's possible that some SIS old-timers might be twisted about that. Especially since even the deputy directors don't have the power and capabilities that Lazlo now has. As for Jenkins—"

"Now that's one suspect who may be harder to nail. From what I see in the file, he has huge clout and connections all the way to the top people in government," Mitch considered out loud.

"So he has power and we're assuming money, but what if

that last assumption is not correct? SNAKE pays quite well. It might be enough to tempt him."

Mitch mulled over Dani's comments, wondering at just how well SNAKE paid. Wondering if someone like Jenkins would succumb to the lure of the cash or if it was something else. "What if Jenkins really does believe Kruger is being unlawfully detained?"

"What if Jenkins is getting the information from SIS, but using it on behalf of his clients?"

"We'll ask Corbett to see what he can find out about Jenkins. In the meantime, we need to try and find out who this mystery SIS agent is."

Dani returned to her computer but didn't sit. Leaning one hand on the tabletop, she scrolled up and down through the profiles of the agents they had identified and shook her head. "None of these agents, clearly. But I suspect that not even Lazlo has the connections to allow us to search the SIS agent files."

"No, he doesn't. But who says we have to get their permission?"

Lucia Cordez was the Lazlo Group's top computer expert and one of the few people aware of the Lazarus Liaison mission. That she had been trusted with that information was a testament to Corbett Lazlo's faith in her. Having asked Lucia to get them access to the SIS agent files, they headed out to dinner, especially since Mitch's stomach rumbled a warning that he was hungry.

Dani was tired and the pain in her side refused to go away, but she relented since she knew the fruit from Uncle Corbett's gift basket wasn't enough to sustain a man like Mitch. You didn't get all that bulk and brawn from fruit.

Hesitant to venture far from the hotel room, she nevertheless realized that a good quick meal and getting into bed for a rest might be just what she needed. She had likely overestimated her readiness for a mission and worried that if things got ugly, she wouldn't be prepared for a fight.

She didn't want to let Mitch down. She had promised to watch his back and she intended to do so.

A few blocks from the hotel, they settled into seats in the alfresco portion of a small local restaurant and quickly opted for the multi-course prix fix dinner. Not only was it the best value, but it boasted a wonderful mix of meats, greens and a dessert table to drool over.

Unlike the night before, conversation was virtually nonexistent during their meal. As Dani watched Mitch ravenously devour the dishes placed before him, as well as some of what she left on her plate, she wondered whether his thoughts were on the case.

Even as she mentally reviewed Kruger's assorted comments and the various reasons why their possible suspects would betray country and honor, her attention was drawn back to Mitch and the fact that he was still alive. Sitting across from her, hale and hearty. Gorgeously hale and hearty.

How many times had she dreamed of such a thing? Imagined the possibility of being with him again?

And here he was, beyond the wildest of her expectations. Beyond logic and reason.

Mitch was alive.

Her heart did a funny, almost painful lurch, and she picked up her hand and pressed against the spot.

Mitch tracked the movement with his gaze and laid down his fork, concern etched into his expression. "Are you okay?"

"I'm fine," she replied, looked away to her plate and

resumed eating the rather tasty veal saltimbocca, although by now, she was quite full after the preceding courses.

Mitch appeared unappeased. "You'd tell me if you weren't, wouldn't you?"

Would she? Dani wondered. Would her ego allow her to admit to weakness? To needing his help? The answer came too quickly, raising another source of concern.

"Yes, I would. We're partners."

"Right. Partners," he said, but the words were clipped. Almost angry. Had he changed his mind? Did he want there to be something else between them?

That thought stayed in her mind throughout the remainder of their meal, raising the specter of where the rest of the night might go if she allowed whatever it was that lingered between them to take its natural course.

When they left the restaurant, she stepped next to Mitch and beneath the shelter of the arm he wrapped around her shoulders. Eased against his side and matched her steps to his, the action making their hips bump together occasionally as they strolled back to the hotel.

The night was hot, with just enough humidity to make being that close to Mitch a trifle warm. The heat between their bodies grew with each step and yet she remained close, the proximity creating a sense of rightness that overrode any discomfort. Besides, she told herself, they were newlyweds and were supposed to be doing newlywed things.

Which prompted her to pause at the door to their room and look up at him. Raise her hand and run it through the longer strands of his hair, still a trifle flat from the weight of the wig he had donned earlier in the day.

Mitch leaned one hand on the wall behind her and moved close. The heat of the night was replaced by the heat of his body. Her breath became his in the limited space he allowed her between him and the wall, but she didn't protest. If anything, Dani suddenly wanted to see where this would go.

After all, she had imagined being with him again thousands, no possibly millions of times in the three years she had thought him dead.

Dropping her hand, she cradled his jaw. Shifted her thumb to trace the defined edges of his full lips. Lips that were warm and moist beneath her finger as he opened his mouth slightly and tongued the pad of her thumb.

"You taste…incredible," he said and laid his hand over hers. Inched her palm to his mouth, where he placed a kiss dead center.

"Is this wise, Mitch? Are we just asking—"

"For problems?" After he said that, he laid his hand at her waist and inched it beneath the hem of the black T-shirt she had slipped into after the interrogation.

The rough palm of his hand rubbed against skin damp from the humidity. She imagined it elsewhere. Her nipples hardened immediately from the thought and at the center of her she grew moist. She didn't want to worry about all the reasons why this might not be logical anymore. She was more Action Girl, anyway.

"Touch me, Mitch."

He groaned and his hand jumped against the flat muscles of her belly for a millisecond before he began his ascent, tracking his hand upward to the front snap of her bra as if aware that she wouldn't settle for anything less than skin-to-skin contact.

With a deft twist, the bra popped open and he slipped his hand beneath and over her breast. Cradled the weight of it in his hand before finding the hard tip of it with his long, strong fingers.

He dragged his thumb across her peaked nipple and then encircled it between thumb and forefinger, rotating the hard tip. Ripping a pleased gasp from her and more moistness between her legs.

He shifted an inch closer, his big body blocking anyone's view of what was happening up against the wall of the building in the very open and public courtyard. Not that Dani cared. All she wanted was him at that moment.

A moment she seemed to have been waiting a lifetime for.

She raised her arm and gripped his shoulder, urging him closer, but Mitch held his ground. She would have protested, only, as his free hand slipped to the button of her jeans, she understood the why of his hesitation.

For once, she wasn't about to argue with him.

The button slipped free easily. The zipper went down with a rasping noise that seemed too loud in the quiet night.

"Mitch?" she questioned, wondering if it wasn't time to take this inside.

"I can't wait anymore, Dani," he muttered as he leaned his forehead against hers and they both watched him ease his hand beneath the denim and cup the center of her. He found her wet and somehow managed to slip one finger inside.

Her breath came in sharp little pants as he stroked her core while still pleasuring her breast with his fingers. She could come just from what he was doing, but it wasn't enough. After so long, nothing but having Mitch inside her, beside her, would satisfy.

She managed to drag the key to the room from his jeans pocket, pausing to caress the erection imprisoned there as she did so. Thanked years of training to get out of tight spots— not that anyone had ever proposed a scenario such as this one—which allowed her to find the lock, slip in the key and open the door even as her knees were starting to grow weak from the passion overtaking her body.

They stumbled through the opening of the door, Mitch's hands still pleasuring her. The door slammed behind them as Mitch kicked it with his foot and they edged ever closer to the bed in the center of the room, heedless of security or caution. The only mission of concern right at that moment was long-denied satisfaction.

The backs of her thighs bumped the edge of the bed, and she stopped, glanced up at Mitch, who likewise paused and moved his hands to her waist.

"Dani?"

The loud ring of the cell phone intruded, persistent with demand.

Mitch ripped it off his belt and answered. "Lama here."

Annoyance. Frustration. Determination. Those three emotions surged through her, but the last lingered, driving her to action.

She laid the leather knapsack holding her laptop and disks on the floor by the bed, watching as Mitch likewise rid himself of his burden. Reaching for the hem of her T-shirt, she dragged it over her head, taking the bra with it, baring herself to his gaze.

He stumbled over his words. "Dani and I…"

Inching her hand over his, she depressed the button for the speaker phone. "Were working on something difficult," she finished for him, slipped the phone from his hand and tossed it on the bed.

"Anything I can help with?" Lazlo asked, his voice echoing slightly over the speaker.

Dani slipped her hands to the waistband of her jeans and with her gaze locked with Mitch's, slowly lowered them to the ground while calmly replying, "I think Mitch and I can handle this ourselves."

"Yes, Corbett. We can do this quite well on our own."

As if to prove his point to the disembodied voice, he cradled her breast and dragged his thumb across the tip of it, dragging a rough groan from her.

Mitch bent his head and tongued the hard tip. She stifled another moan and somehow managed to say, "Mitch and I will give you a full report in the morning."

"In the morning then. Carry on." *Click.*

Against her breast came Mitch's amused chuckle a second before he stood upright again.

"Carry on? Do you think we should consider that an order?" he said, a wry smile on his face even as he brought one big hand up to cradle her rib cage, right at the spot she had been rubbing earlier and where a dull ache lingered.

The ache transferred itself to her heart, awakening doubt about the wisdom of continuing. "You and I always follow orders, don't we?"

Mitch sensed the change that overtook her in the strain that entered her body. "This isn't about orders or a mission, Dani. It's about us."

"Us? Is there an us? Can there be an us after…"

"The past? After the lies?" He dropped his hand and stepped away, as if realizing the moment had passed. Realizing that he had almost made one of the biggest mistakes of his life—besides trusting her in the first place.

"I'm sorry. I can't—"

Dani didn't wait to hear more. She snatched up her shirt to cover herself and fled to the bathroom.

Chapter 9

The chill of the tile bathed her naked backside but was nothing compared to the biting disappointment enveloping her body. Her heart.

She had been stupid to let desire get the better of her. She should have known better.

Mitch knocked on the door. "Dani."

Duh, she thought. Who else could it be in the bathroom, feeling like an idiot? Feeling like something that should be flushed down the toilet.

"I just need a few minutes," she called out and slipped the shirt over her head, both to combat the cold and to attempt to restore some respectability to herself.

She stood, smoothed the shirt down as far as it could go, not that it covered much below her waistline. But it had to be enough.

Whirling on her heel, she walked to the door and yanked it open.

Mitch stood with one arm braced against the bathroom doorjamb, as Dani finally came out.

She pushed past him into the room. At the edge of the bed, she scooped up her jeans and slipped into them before facing him.

"How long before Lucia can give us access to SIS?"

Mitch stalked over. He held out his hands before him, ready to talk about what happened earlier until she crossed her arms against her chest and tilted her head up in challenge. At that, he mumbled a curse and raked a hand through his hair.

"Right. Lucia." He grabbed for the PDA on his belt, cursed again as he realized it wasn't there. It was on the bed. On the bed where just minutes ago she had been on the verge of seducing him.

Realizing that, he leaned over and scooped it up. With a vicious jab of one button, he brought the PDA to his ear and stalked back and forth.

Mitch shot Dani a half glance as he waited for Lucia to pick up. It had been only a couple of hours, probably way too soon for Lucia to have anything for them. Despite that, he hung on for ring after ring until Lucia's voice mail answered.

"Lucia, it's Mitch. Give me a call as soon as you've got something."

Facing Dani, he said, "She's not answering."

"So I guess we just keep on working with what we've got." Dani scooped up her knapsack and took it over to the table, her movements brusque. Efficiently, she set up her equipment. Grabbed the DVDs with the Lazlo Group files and neatly organized everything on the table, ready to toil again.

Mitch wasn't ready for the same. Not physically and not after the emotional roller coaster of the past half hour. "You can work all you want. I'm going to get some rest until Lucia calls."

Dani didn't even bother to turn around. With a shrug, she settled into the chair and the *tap-tap-tap* of her fingers on the keys soon filled the quiet of the room.

Mitch toed off his shoes, leaned back and pillowed his head on his hands, his gaze trained on Dani's stiff back. He had wondered so often during the past three years what drove her, and in the course of just a day or so, he had a better idea of the complexity of her personality. Of the determination that made her embark on a path of justice. A path from which she had detoured with her actions in tempting the Prince of Silvershire to his fate.

He understood the why of it. Could even forgive her role in the prince's death as her heartfelt words ricocheted in his head.

I didn't want another family to suffer like mine did.

He knew she and her sister still harbored a great deal of pain from the murders of their parents. They had been scarred emotionally, and those kinds of scars took a long time to heal. It helped him understand the aloofness he had felt at first around Dani. The distance she had kept until they had come to know one another a little better, although even then, he had sensed there was a part of her she kept from others.

The part of her that had hidden her real identity from him. But also, the part of her that maybe feared he would die and leave her as her parents had done. A fear almost fully realized nearly three years ago.

Guilt swamped him then at the thought of her grief over his supposed death. If he could take back the deception, he would, only…

Did she feel similar regret over her duplicity? If that fateful day in the alley hadn't occurred, would she have continued to deceive him about who she really was?

Toward the end of their time together, he had started to

think he had finally found a home with someone. A place that he wanted to be more than anywhere else.

But she hadn't been what she seemed, and the kind of woman she had been and probably still was didn't seem like the kind of woman who wanted to settle down. She had her own agenda—namely, finding her parents' killers. Not that he had thought of himself as a settling-down kind of guy. But Dani had inspired such thoughts in him.

Damn, he thought, rolling onto his side and away from the sight of her, hoping that by doing so, he could forget about her for a short time. When the light clicks and clacks of her hands on the keyboard continued to filter into his consciousness, he yanked a pillow over his ears, muffling the sound.

Taking deep breaths, he focused on relaxing. On getting some sleep so that when Lucia called, he'd be ready to work and finish this mission.

After all, the faster they finished, the quicker he could get on with his life and forget all about Dani.

Dani told herself to focus on the files and not on the grumpy tossing and turning coming from the bed behind her.

She blocked out the creaks of the bed that sounded with each flip of his big body. Ignored the mumbled curses and sounds of his punching a pillow into flatness.

At least, she tried to.

When it grew silent after some time, she allowed herself a quick glimpse over her shoulder and realized he had drifted off to sleep. Slightly jealous and annoyed that he should find rest while she couldn't, she blew out an exasperated sigh and returned to reviewing the files, certain that they were missing something in the reports they had been provided.

She went back over the list of all the SIS and Lazlo Group

agents and handlers involved in the various operations. Checked off the names of the people they were investigating, all with no luck. Reminded herself that when those clues failed to yield any connections, she had to shift her attention out a degree of separation.

First on her list—the people who had hired the Lazlo Group to undertake each of the investigations that had resulted in an operative's being attacked. The list grew quickly, but as before, no clear connection arose that would raise suspicion. The bulk of the Lazlo clients were seemingly respectable citizens.

Much like Barrett Jenkins, only warning bells were going off that Jenkins was not what he purported to be.

As she skimmed the list of Lazlo clients once again, one name caught her eye—Olivia Alegria. The Lazlo list had few celebrity clients, leaning more toward politicos and the kind of wealthy people who didn't court the press for attention.

Olivia Alegria therefore didn't fit the usual profile of a Lazlo client. She was the widow of a well-known soccer ce-lebrity who had died in a car accident earlier in the year.

As Dani turned her attention to the case file, she realized that Olivia had hired the Lazlo Group to investigate a charitable or-ganization with which her husband had been involved. Accord-ing to the file, Olivia had taken over her dead husband's role as an honorary spokesperson with a lot of determination, but when she grew doubtful about where the funds were going and asked questions that went unanswered, she had turned to the Lazlo Group, wanting to protect her dead husband's memory.

The agent killed in Prague had been involved in that in-vestigation.

When Dani went to the Web site for the foundation, she noted the tribute to Olivia's husband, Sergio Alegria, on the opening page. She surfed through the site, looking for additional information and finally hit pay dirt—one of the foundation's most recent contributions was a nice-sized check to a pet project of none other than John Breckenridge, Barrett Jenkins's most prominent and well-known client. The site boasted a picture of the up-and-coming politician along with a letter of thanks from him.

Mitch and she were going to have to pay a visit to Olivia Alegria and question her about her concerns regarding the foundation and any information she might have on John Breckenridge and his activities.

A soft, barely vibrating buzz snagged Dani's attention.

She turned and noticed the light flashing on the PDA still firmly glued to Mitch's hip. She wondered why he didn't hear or feel the vibration.

Rising, and intent on not disturbing him since he seemed dead to the world, she walked to his side and laid her hand on the PDA.

A major mistake she quickly realized.

Before she could react Mitch snared her hand and flipped her up and over his side and onto the bed. He followed up by straddling her body and pinning her arms above her head, imprisoning her beneath him.

Beneath his very hard and very aroused body, she realized.

Damn, Mitch thought as reality replaced the instinctive defense behavior with which he had reacted when he sensed the touch at his hip.

His hip, where his PDA vibrated angrily, demanding his attention.

But his attention was on Dani's body beneath his. On her breasts, rising and falling with her slightly quickened breath. On her face, which at first reflected surprise over his actions and then slowly changed, until it was obvious she had noted his physical state.

The state he was in because he had been dreaming about her.

Snagging the PDA with one hand while releasing Dani's arms, he shot a quick look at the display before answering. Lucia, finally.

"I hope you have some good news for me," he said and watched as Dani rubbed at her wrists where he had grabbed them, but made no motion to shift from beneath him.

"Nothing yet. As expected, SIS has quite a few security barriers in place around their network. Corbett and I are working on it."

Mitch stifled a chuckle but couldn't resist baiting Lucia, who had always been a good friend to him and Aidan. "Corbett and you, is it? Maybe you'd be more focused if you worked on your own."

Lucia's husky laugh chased across the phone line. "And maybe you should consider taking advantage of this time with Dani after waiting for her for so long."

Possibly waiting too long, he thought as the line went dead.

He gazed down at Dani's face and battled the urge to kiss her lips. Pick up where they had stopped earlier.

"Mitch?" Dani questioned at his delay.

"Lucia hasn't been able to get in yet." He paused, uncertain whether to continue with his friend's message, but then decided there was nothing to lose—except maybe his sanity.

"She thinks I should stop wasting time with you."

Frown lines marred Dani's forehead. "Why would she think… Oh. She wants you and me—"

"*I* want you and me to deal with this. With what we feel," he admitted.

Desire for certain. It had been there before and had risen

again as his body pressed hers down into the bed. Memories flooded back of the many times they had made love.

She reached up to cradle his jaw. "I won't deny I'm still attracted to you. Physically."

His lips thinned into a tight line. If the physical was all they had now... "I want you as well. So I guess there's nothing stopping us from satisfying that want, is there?"

Chapter 10

Was there? Dani wondered as she examined him above her. Alive and breathing.

For so long she had dreamed of him being back in her life, only she had never expected that it would be like this. With lies and deceit tainting the something special they had shared the year they were together in Rome.

With death having nearly claimed both of them.

Nearly being the operative word. They weren't dead. They were both alive. Alive and clearly still attracted to one another. Only she wasn't sure if what she felt for him was real anymore or if she had built up their year together into something that wasn't quite what it had been.

And if it *had* been as wonderful as she remembered? Could they find a way to forget all the bad that had happened between them and recapture what they had once felt? Did she even want to?

"Dani?" Mitch pressed at her hesitation.

So many questions and yet she knew only one certain thing—better to be damned for trying to find the answers than running away and never knowing what might have happened if she had taken a chance.

She answered him with a kiss, soft at first, against those unyielding lips. Inviting him gently to go with her. To share in the passion that still simmered between them, if only for a few hours.

Beneath the urging of her mouth, his gradually relaxed. The muscles of his body loosened as he allowed himself to respond to her kiss. To the way she nearly ate him up, as if he was the only form of sustenance that could nourish her.

Maybe he was. Maybe the bleakness of her life in the past three years was all due to his absence.

She refused to consider how it would be if he left again at the end of their mission.

As he shifted his body to the side, she took advantage of her freedom and rolled, bringing him beneath her. It let her capture his face in her hands, cradle his strong jaw as she kept on kissing him, her mouth opening on his. Tracing the outline of his lips with her tongue. Biting and sucking at his lower lip and welcoming the thrust of his tongue into her mouth until it wasn't enough.

She sat up slightly and sucked in a rough breath, trying to rein in the hammering beat of her heart.

Mitch met Dani's gaze and inhaled slowly, needing control when what he wanted to do more than anything was rip off all her clothes and take her. Hard. Fast. Tenderly. Slowly. Hell, he just wanted her over and over and over again until his body refused to work anymore.

Using his greater strength, he surged back and sat up

against the headboard, Dani firmly settled in his lap and against his erection. His mouth never left hers, except to gulp in the occasional breath and even then, it seemed like too much time away from her.

When she flexed her hips, driving herself tighter against him, he groaned and moved his head down to the crook of her neck.

She cupped the back of his head with one hand while yanking his T-shirt from his pants. When she slipped her hand beneath to stroke his side, a shudder ripped through him.

"Mitch?"

"Don't stop, Dani. I want your hands on me. All over me," he said and she complied, dragging the shirt up and over his head and laying her hands on his shoulders.

He met her gaze then, and knew she wanted the same, but first he had to have a taste.

Bending his head again, he licked at the spot at the crook of her neck and followed up with a gentle love bite. It dragged a shocked sharp breath from her, but she urged him on.

"Bite me again," she said while she moved her free hand across his shoulder. Dipped it down and cupped the swell of his chest.

He bit down again lightly. Licked the spot playfully, eliciting a quick laugh from her. Then he began to suck, gently at first, but then more forcefully and as he did so, Dani moved her hips in a matching rhythm. Moaned as he pulled hard enough to bruise her skin.

Marked her as his, he realized and his erection swelled painfully with the thought. She *was* his. Well, at least for now, and he knew just what she liked. What she wanted, and he told her.

"I want to taste you," he said, grabbing the neck of her T-shirt and with one powerful tug, exposing her breasts with their rock-hard tips.

Fulfilling his desire, he brought his mouth to one peaked nipple and took it into his mouth while pleasuring the other with his fingers. She tasted both sweet and salty from the light sweat covering her body.

She tasted like Dani, a unique essence he craved beyond belief.

"I can't get enough of you," he said and moved his mouth to her other breast, sucking and biting. Rotating the wet peak with his fingers.

Dani dragged in a shaky breath and dug her fingers into the hard muscles of Mitch's shoulders, trying to steady a world quickly spinning out of control as his actions and words made her so wet and needy that she was almost ready to come.

She didn't want to rush. And she wanted to pleasure him. Touch every inch. Taste every millimeter of hard muscle. Suck him into her mouth and feel him swell and jerk beneath her lips.

She applied gentle pressure to his shoulders, slipping out of his lap and earning a protest from him until he realized her intent. Then his hands were quickly helping hers to undo his jeans and drag them down his legs until he lay naked before her.

As she had thought, he was more muscular, with every line of his body cleanly chiseled. She kneeled beside him and laid her hand on his abdomen. Traced the long thin line from his navel upward where the knife had bitten deep into him. Bending, she replaced her hand with her mouth, kissing the length of the scar and then continuing upward, until she was at a spot right above his heart.

She dropped another kiss there, ripping a groan from him. "Dani. I—"

She covered his mouth with her hand and shook her head.

"No words. No promises. Nothing but pleasure this time, Mitch," she said, because she had suddenly grown afraid that she was giving him too much and there would be nothing left of her when it was over.

Mitch's mouth hardened into a tight line, and then he erupted, pinning her to the mattress. His naked body pressed against her, rough. Almost punishing at first, until his grasp gentled and the harsh lines on his face relaxed.

"Just pleasure, then," he said and dropped his head down to the line of her collarbone. Slipped his tongue along that ridge and then downward, to her breasts again, where he suckled her. Alternating his hands and mouth until she was drenched and writhing against the bed, needing more.

He rose up then, made short work of removing her jeans. He paused, however, shot her a look and urged her to her side before turning his body so that they were nestled together, his head near her center, her lips close to his throbbing erection.

Dani licked the tip of him as he found the center of her and kissed the pleasure-swollen nub. When he eased his fingers into her, she nearly came, but fought it back and took him into her mouth.

He was hard and thick. Salty. As she sucked at him she wrapped her hand around him, stroked, cupped him with her other hand and caressed him.

He groaned and expelled a breath she felt against her dampness, but then he brought his mouth to her center once more. Sucked at the nub while he did something with his fingers that had her moaning and clenching her muscles around him.

He jerked against her lips and she tasted the first hint of his release. His body tensed as he reined himself in and she eased back, slowed her caresses because when he came, she wanted it to be inside her. She wanted to come with him, her body tight around his.

As if he read her mind, he moved suddenly, shifting back around so that they were face-to-face again, both breathing heavily as they battled desire and themselves.

Mitch bent his head and kissed her. A gentle whisper against her lips. A nuzzle of his nose across her cheek before he laid a hand on her waist and urged her body close to his.

Warmth bathed the length of her. Comforting, welcoming warmth. She surrendered to it. To the peace that surrounded her as he brought his arms around her and she embraced him.

It was only a moment, although it felt like an eternity. Then he kissed her again with a little more demand. Cupped her breast and caressed her nipple while holding her close with the arm snaked down her back.

She opened her mouth to him and eased her tongue within as she slipped her hand down his body. He was wet from her mouth and that first loss of control. The slickness let her slide her hand against him as she stroked, building his desire until she felt the familiar jerk and his groan came against her breast.

"Dani. I want to be inside you. Are you—"

"It's okay. I haven't…"

She didn't want to admit there hadn't been anyone else in the nearly three years since she'd thought him dead. The confession would possibly give him too much power, but it slipped from her lips.

"There's been no one else."

Something ripped through Mitch's body with her words. Then his own telling confession warmed her. "It was only you, Dani. Only you."

He rolled her beneath him and eased in. She gasped at his

possession, taken aback by the wonder of their joining. By the rightness of how she fit around him. Beneath him.

Something flickered in his gaze as she held onto him. When he finally began to move, his thrusts were gentle at first, as if hesitant. As if she were a virgin and needed tenderness and she considered that wasn't so far off the money.

Like that first taking, this union could bring them immense satisfaction, but possibly even greater pain.

She refused to consider the latter at that moment. For three years she had wished for Mitch to be alive again and in her arms. Now that he was, she wouldn't let any other thoughts interfere.

She raised herself up so she could kiss his lips and urge him on. "That feels good, Mitch. Don't stop, love."

Beneath her hands, his muscles clenched and his next words exploded from his mouth against her lips. "God, Dani. It's been too long."

Cradling his head in her hands, she whispered, "Don't hold back on me, Mitch. Not after all this time."

She kissed him then, opening her mouth against his and imitating the thrusts of his body with her tongue until they were both winded and on the edge. She dropped back down onto the bed and raised her knees, cradling his hips as he pumped into her, harder and slightly rougher, dragging a gasp from her as her passion peaked. With one more rough thrust, she came, calling out his name and holding onto his shoulders as her body arched up off the bed and shook with the force of her release.

But he wasn't done yet, it seemed.

Mitch's arms trembled as he braced them on the bed and watched Dani's release. Felt the sensation of it gripping him. Pulling him inward. He forced his eyes closed for a second, savoring her body's response. The soft little cries spilling from her mouth and the way her fingers dug into the muscles of his shoulders.

He felt himself swell and tighten as his own release neared, but he battled it back. It had been way too long, and he didn't want the moment to end.

As her body calmed a bit, he bent his head and suckled her nipples, arousing her yet again. Earning a playful moan of satisfaction from her.

"I guess you like," he teased and nipped the edge of one nipple with his teeth.

Dani, being Dani, was not one to just lie there.

One second he was above her, and the next she had rolled, bringing him beneath her. Deepening his penetration as she sat back on him, yanking a groan from him.

"So I guess you like, too," she joked and shifted her hips, riding him.

He cupped her breasts, strumming the tight peaks of her nipples. Urging her on not just because it felt good, but because he knew she needed to be the one in control right now and he didn't mind. He'd never minded, it occurred to him as he gave his body over to her.

When he finally lost control, he called her name and she followed him, releasing his with a sharp cry.

Their bodies were trembling as she dropped down onto him, her body covered in a fine sheen of sweat, as was his.

A second later he heard the muffled ring of his PDA and felt the vibration beneath the covers directly below his butt.

Fumbling to recover the PDA from the tangle of sheets, he slipped out of Dani, earning a protest from her and a quick kiss on his cheek as she snuggled against his side. Rather possessively, she tossed a thigh over his, laid one hand on his chest and played with his nipple, possibly intending that their interlude continue.

He answered the phone. "Lama, here."

"I'm in," Lucia said.

Chapter 11

He groaned at her announcement. He mouthed "I'm sorry," to Dani, then said to Lucia, "I'm putting you on speaker phone."

Dani nodded, understanding that it was time to go back to business. Before she did, she leaned close and brushed a quick kiss across his cheek. Then she eased from his side, collected her T-shirt and slipped that on.

"What can you tell us?" she asked as she searched the floor for her jeans.

"I've set up a computer here that will allow you access to SIS. It will change its IP address at random intervals, but even with that, you can't linger for long, so make your access time count," Lucia advised them. Over the speaker phone, Dani heard the *click-clack* of nails on a keyboard.

"Great. How will we get to that PC?" Mitch asked as she finally located her jeans beneath the bed and put them back on.

"You've got the remote connection software on both your

laptops. I'll send a link that will get you to the computer and an automated log-in script I've created. Get in and get out as quickly as possible." She signed off, leaving Dani staring at Mitch as he sat on the edge of the bed, staring at her.

"Dani, I…" His slate eyes turned a turbulent gray and she held up her hand.

"Let's not, Mitch. Not right now." She wanted to hold on to the moment for just a little longer. Imagine that the pleasure in his arms could be something more than just pleasure, since their interlude had proved to her one thing—it hadn't just been her imagination all these years.

They were wonderful together physically. But she knew it took more than that for there to be anything lasting. And you didn't build something lasting in just a few hours. That would take time and trust.

Mitch clenched his teeth, anger surging through him until he met her gaze. He saw something there. Something that said things had definitely changed. Could they ever be the same again?

Only time would tell, he thought as he nodded and turned his attention to breaking into SIS.

Auburn curls caressed his abdomen as the young woman sought to satisfy him, her mouth expert as one might expect from someone paid to earn their living this way.

Troy tried to focus on that expertise, willing his mind and body to accept the pleasure of her caresses, but release eluded him as did peace. His mind was too engaged in reviewing the snatches of conversation he had overheard earlier that night.

From beside his bed came a sharp beep—a call coming into his mother's private line.

He had managed to rig the phone system to alert him, but

tapping into the line had been too risky. His mother expected that others would attempt to secure sensitive information and regularly had their top experts sweep her office and other public areas for all kinds of surveillance equipment.

But the last place she would expect to be watched would be in her bedroom. Especially by her own son, and Troy knew that if he was to one day head their organization, he had to be even more ruthless and cunning than Cassandra. Rumor had it that was how she had risen to the top. Troy often discounted the gossip, however, which also included rumors that she had been the one who had killed her own father. He didn't want to believe his mother could do that, but maybe being ruthless had eaten away enough of her soul that she had. The way he felt, the guilt for what he'd done eating away at his soul.

Pushing away the young woman, who began to protest until he reached into the nightstand and tossed a wad of bills at her, he stalked over to the desk at one side of his bedroom and with a flick of his finger on the touchpad, pulled his laptop from standby mode.

A quick click and his mother's bedroom came into view.

She sat on the edge of the bed, phone in hand while a handsome silver-haired man spooned against her back, his hand at her breast.

His mother had also been interrupted in the midst of pleasure.

He smiled as Cassandra elbowed the man and with an abrupt shake of her head, instructed him to leave. He did so without delay, probably well aware of the penalties for displeasing the mercurial Cassandra.

Like mother like son, Troy thought, knowing that in their lives business always came before pleasure.

His mother rose from the bed, magnificently naked, her body amazingly toned and fit for a woman in her mid-forties. She could easily pass for much younger, he thought, and turned his attention to her clearly annoyed conversation with whoever was on the other end of the line.

"They've moved him to Rome?" she said, striding arrogantly before her bed, her auburn hair shifting across her body as she did so.

Kruger, he thought, realizing this was the follow-up phone call to the disturbing conversation from the day before. It occurred to him that Kruger had been caught in Rome, and he wondered at the significance of his being returned there once again.

"Who's working on this assignment for Lazlo?" Cassandra asked and clearly didn't like the answer she received. She stopped and raked her hair back in agitation.

"Two agents? Is Corbet afraid just one of his precious people isn't enough?" she said, excitement dragging out the sounds of her native French in her speech. Before the person on the other end of the line could respond, she continued. "Do we know who they are? What they want with Kruger?"

Lazlo's investigations into Kruger had been inconsequential in the scheme of things, Troy thought. They had already dispatched the Sparrow to take care of the man. And then they had dispatched of the Sparrow.

"What you don't know could be harmful for us," Cassandra said, the tones of her voice cold and cutting, her accent growing thicker with her agitation. Troy knew her well enough to guess at what would follow.

"We need to get rid of Kruger. As soon as possible. Do you know where the two agents are located?"

His mother flopped down on the edge of the bed, annoyance evident in every line of her body as she waited for an answer, but it took some time. He wondered whether her inside source was busy trying to convince her otherwise or making excuses for his lack of information.

The latter he discovered as his mother curtly said, "Find them. We'll kill them, too."

Interesting, he thought. His mother's little mole clearly had some problems with getting information, and that whole issue was making Cassandra rather unhappy.

Troy was tired of his mother's sullen moods and her constant babying. If he was to one day head their family business, he needed to be able to deal with situations like these.

Wanting to show his mother he could take care of things, Troy picked up the phone, intending to do just that.

His tech guru answered on the first ring, knowing that he didn't like to be kept waiting.

"Good evening, Mr. Dumont."

"Something's up. I need you to break into the Lazlo system."

The man's gulp was audible across the phone line. "Sir, their top person's really good. She'll have all kinds of traps and alerts to let her know if someone tries to do it."

He didn't need the man to tell him that. He was well aware of the strength of Lazlo security. It was their business after all. "What about their e-mail system?" he asked, thinking it might yield better results.

Although a well-secured system forced periodic changes, people were sometimes predictable. Family names and dates. Pets. Post-it notes on keyboards or monitors.

"I'll try, sir. That's all I can promise," the man said and hurriedly hung up to begin his assignment.

Troy suspected it would be futile. While some people might be careless, Corbett Lazlo didn't strike him as the careless sort, and anyone that far up in his organization wouldn't be either. He suspected they would be by the book and thorough. Plus, they had likely set up some kind of warning system to alert them when someone accessed their accounts via the Internet.

It would be hard work to uncover Lazlo's latest mission, but excitement rose in him at the thought. Maybe this time he could prove to his mother that he was ready.

With Mitch at the keyboard, Dani ran down the information they had from Kruger about the suspect SIS agent. "Average height. Light brown hair. Light-colored eyes. Mid-twenties. Sharp dresser. Gold signet ring with the letter *T*." Dani paused for a second and then said, "But with some engraved scripts, a *J* might be mistaken for a *T*."

Mitch clicked on the link Lucia had provided, and a few seconds later they were in. Mindful of Lucia's earlier admonitions, Mitch quickly searched on both surnames and first names beginning with *J*, trusting Dani's judgment. He printed out the basic results and then cut the connection.

Dani took the papers from the small portable printer and laid them on the table between them. Out of the many entries, they limited the field to nearly two dozen based on age and race. With search time possibly being limited before their intrusion was detected, they tightened those two dozen even further to the eight closest to Kruger's description.

Mitch once again logged on and quickly printed out the basic bios on all eight of the employees. They split up the list, and each sat down to review the possible suspects.

Dani flipped through the pages, considering the ranks of the agents as well as their assignments to determine whether they would have had access to someone as high level as

Kruger. As she went from one page to another, some of the faces were familiar from her time at SIS. She had actually worked with one of the agents on an earlier assignment. She had passed others on occasion during her time in both the London and the Rome offices.

Although she had masqueraded as the Sparrow as part of the high-level assignment, to most within the organization she was just another field agent.

It troubled her that the mole might be someone she knew or had even worked with. Someone who had sworn to protect both country and the other agents with whom they labored. Someone responsible now for four deaths and the injuries to her and Mitch.

She rubbed at the soreness in her side. It struck home now more than before that her injuries were possibly courtesy of a fellow agent.

"You okay?" Mitch asked from beside her. He was back at work on the computer, probably already researching one of the possible suspects.

"I guess. When you first said that someone at SIS might have outed me…it didn't seem real. Now," she said, motioning to the pictures of all the men scattered on the table, "it's a little too real."

"Betrayal is a bitter thing."

Dani winced at his comment, but he quickly tried to cover for it. "I wasn't talking about us. It's about one of them and what they did."

"Right," she said, unconvinced, and returned to her analysis of the possible suspects, although something made her initially set aside those familiar to her. Total avoidance, she acknowledged.

She was down to her last unfamiliar face when something

struck her about the man in the photo. No, make that every-thing struck her about the man in the photo. He was very handsome. Possibly in a way that Kruger might think of as pretty. Strong jaw and well-shaped, full lips.

Truly kissable lips, she thought, admiring his mouth and the strong chin below with a perfect cleft in its center. Straight nose, not too pug or sharp. Eyes…green the bio said, not that it was possible to tell from the photo taken.

The bio indicated light brown for his hair color, and she guessed at sandy-brown although it appeared darker in the photo.

Sharp dresser according to Kruger. From mid-chest up, her suspect appeared to be just that. The suit was sharply pressed and fitted just so across broad shoulders. Bright white shirt with nary a wrinkle and a tie with a modern but pleasing pattern.

"Got something?" Mitch asked and leaned close. He wrinkled his nose at the photo and mumbled, "I think the Brits would say nancy boy."

Dani chuckled and found it impossible not to tease him. "Nancy boy? I think he's rather attractive. He's the right age."

Mitch grunted. "Right. What about the bio?"

"Didn't get there yet," she said, prompting another Nean-derthal like grunt from Mitch, this one coupled with a shrug.

"Stop drooling over the nancy boy and get to it, then. Night's almost over."

The annoyance in his voice was clear and for a moment she wondered if he was jealous that she found the agent attrac-tive. Glancing at her watch, she realized he was right about the night being over. It was nearly three in the morning. While she used to be able to go for a few days straight without rest, that was no longer true. The demands of the past couple of days were telling. Her body ached, particularly near her injury. She suspected she had pulled something while training the other day, but had had no time to baby herself.

Physically she was tired. Emotionally she was battered. So much had happened in such a short time. Mitch's reappearance. The possible SIS betrayal.

Making love to him.

She forced herself to acknowledge that it had been just sex. Truly satisfying, mattress-denting sex, but just sex and not love. Not yet. Maybe never.

Armed with that decision and the bio of the nancy boy—one Jared Williams—she logged onto the Lazlo network and began running Williams through the assorted databases.

The night was growing short and temptation sat at her side, occasionally bumping elbows with her as they worked together. At one point she glanced over at him and their gazes met, locked for longer than necessary.

Was he imagining getting back into bed together? Making love once again?

When he turned away to look back at his monitor, she drew in a shaky sigh and with hands that trembled, forced herself to work.

Failure wasn't an option on this mission. As she worked, it occurred to her that she couldn't make a mistake about Mitch again either—it had been too painful to lose him the first time around.

She didn't think it would be any easier this time.

Chapter 12

It seemed like she had no sooner put her head down on the pillow than the alarm was going off, calling them to rise and head out for their mission.

Mitch surprised her by being up already and having a large triple espresso waiting for her. She didn't bother with sugar, just belted it back even before a quick shower.

By the time they had packed up their equipment and put on all of their disguises, absent the wigs, the caffeine had made up a bit for barely two hours of sleep. Jumping on the tram, they headed toward the Via Condotti but only got about two-thirds of the way there when traffic came to a halt. Way up ahead of them, clearly visible through the windshield, a plume of dark smoke rose from the skyline close to their destination.

Conjecture and gossip immediately sprung up among the riders on the tram, but as Dani met Mitch's gaze, it was clear that he was thinking much the same thing she was—something bad had happened at Lazlo's Rome offices.

With traffic stalled, the conductor offered to let the riders off. As she and Mitch jumped onto the curb, Mitch's PDA began to ring.

"It's Corbett," Mitch said and stepped into a tight alcove in the wall of one building. Dani wedged herself beside him to try to hear as Mitch answered.

Snatches of Lazlo's report filtered to her over the street noise and the wail of a siren heading toward the fire.

"Lost communications just a short while ago."

"Haven't been able to reach anyone."

Mitch met her gaze and nodded. "Dani and I are heading there immediately. We'll give a full report once we determine what's occurred."

"Careful….mission possibly compromised," was all she heard before Mitch ended the call.

"Let's roll," he said and in double-time, they raced to the Lazlo building.

Troy watched the fire from a few doors down, satisfaction on his face. As the crowd ebbed and flowed, Troy moved with it until he found himself almost directly across the street from the burning building, a small alley behind him.

Something hard jabbed him in the middle of the back. He knew better than to ignore it when a hand landed on his right shoulder and eased him into the alley. As they moved farther and farther back, the hard object shifted upward from the middle of his back until the cold metal of the gun pressed against a spot beneath his left ear.

"Mommy send you to make sure I did the job right?" the man said, his voice low and rough against Troy's ear. With his free hand, the man patted him down and swiftly discovered the Glock in the holster beneath his left arm.

"Just came to give you some help," Troy explained as the assassin pulled the Glock from the holster and held the gun out where he could see it. Giving it a little toss, he chuckled and said, "Baby gun for a baby boy."

Troy knew men like this only understood one thing. He snagged the gun back from the other man's grasp and faced him. He was a brutish type, his nose crooked and a jagged scar along one brow. "I came to give you information."

"Baby boy's got balls after all," the man said, tucking his weapon into his holster. He crossed his thick-muscled arms against a massive chest and eyeballed him. "What kind of info could you possibly give me?"

"The location of the two agents," Troy said and calmly re-holstered his Glock.

"How do you—"

The assassin's cell phone sounded and he answered, but said nothing. He only listened as Troy mouthed the name of the hotel.

Albergo Santa Carmela.

With a nod, the man shut off the cell phone. "Think I can't handle this by myself?"

Troy shrugged. "I'm sure you can, but won't another pair of hands make the job go faster?"

The man laughed, throwing his head back. His body shook with his amusement.

Heat flared across Troy's face. Whipping out his gun, he stuck it under the man's jaw and drove him roughly against the wall. "Don't mess with me because I won't hesitate to kill you."

"Crazy bastard just like your mother."

Crazy? No, just tired of not being taken seriously. Of being treated like a child. Plus, a killer like this only respected one thing—greater strength. "We go together. I want an end to this business with Lazlo. Understood?"

The man grunted his answer. "Understood. We've got one man, one woman. Woman's a looker with short black hair. Long brown on the man. Big and muscular with a tattoo Kruger said."

"What else did he say?" Troy asked, jamming the gun up into the man's jaw.

"Please, please don't, mate." His voice was pitched high like a girl's in imitation of Kruger before he lowered it once again and said, "Then he crapped his pants."

Troy laughed and released him. "Kruger always was a little bugger. Let's go finish this."

Destroyed. The Lazlo offices had taken a major hit. Besides the fire, a portion of the building had collapsed, Dani realized.

"We need to let Corbett know," Mitch said and dialed his cell phone.

Dani nodded, standing beside him at the doorway to a small notions shop. There were crowds all around, eager for a view of what had happened. As on the bus, conjecture filled the air.

"A terrorist attack."

"Heard it was a gas explosion."

"Some man killed his wife and then set the whole place on fire."

Mitch laid a hand on her arm and urged her a step back into the alcove for the door so that they might have some privacy. With his back to the crowd, he turned on the speaker in the PDA and held it between them.

"You've got info?" Mitch said.

"We've tapped into an Italian news feed. It looks quite bad," Lazlo said.

"The upper levels have been destroyed. Fire and some kind of collapse," Dani advised.

"What about the main Lazlo offices below ground?" Mitch asked, although she suspected like him that the answer would not be good.

"We lost all communication with them about an hour ago. Lucia is trying to reestablish some kind of line."

"We're heading back to the safe house until we decide what our next step is," Mitch said.

Annoyance flared through Dani at Mitch's unilateral decision, and when he disconnected, she said, "What makes you think that's where I want to go?"

Surprise flared across his features. "What's up with you?"

"We're a team. We make decisions together."

"The safe house is the best bet until we know more," Mitch insisted.

"If they knew enough to attack this building, what makes you think the hotel is any safer?" She put her arms on her hips and looked up at him, defiance in every line of her body.

He once again whipped out his PDA. "We can check it out via the surveillance—"

She laid a hand over his as it held the device and in softer tones said, "There's only so much the cameras will tell us. The rest we need to do."

He looked away, up the street toward the burning building. His hand tensed beneath hers. "Mitch?" she asked, wondering at what she was reading as hesitation.

He nailed her with his gaze. "Are you ready for this? For a full-out battle to the death? Because that's what this is."

Her initial reaction might have been anger that he doubted her readiness and willingness, but she sensed he asked because he wasn't necessarily sure about himself and because he was concerned for her. "I always thought I was, but when I was holding you in my arms, praying that you wouldn't die…"

He cradled her cheek, tenderness in his touch and a tremble of fear. "I don't want to risk you again, but—"

"We have a job to do. We have to end this so we can have our lives back." So that they could rise up like Lazarus, possibly into a world without the violence and death of this one. So she could see her sister Lizzy Bee again.

She didn't dare wonder if the future held a place for her and Mitch together.

Mitch dropped his hand, his face grim. "So if they know where we might go, we need to be ready. Maybe even plan a surprise of our own."

She nodded. "What kinds of tricks do you have in your bag?"

Lucia had managed to establish contact with the server holding the feeds from the various surveillance cameras in the Rome offices. The report she gave them was grim, Mitch thought, as he and Dani ducked into a small street just a few blocks from the hotel.

"We have one shooter going in. Killed the two security guards and the Lazlo operative inside before finding Kruger. After that the man planted several explosive devices in both our offices and the building above."

"Thorough," Mitch said and then asked, "What can you tell us about the shooter?"

"Approximately six foot four. Muscular. No way to tell race since his face was covered," Lucia advised.

"What kind of firepower are we facing?" Dani asked.

"Uzi. At least two handguns, one of them a Glock from the looks of it. Probably hollow points or military grade ammo. We can't confirm yet if it's the same shooter as before."

Dani looked up at him, but any earlier fear or hesitation had been replaced by steely determination. Her warrior's face. She was prepped for battle. "Got it, Lucia, and thanks."

"Be careful out there," the other woman said before signing off.

"Not much to go on." Mitch tucked his PDA back onto his belt, put his hands on his hips and peered down the narrow street. Just a few blocks, minutes away, and the assassin might be waiting for them.

But just one against their two. "I'll go in first," he said.

"No, I will. Being male, he'll assume I'm an easy take-down. It might make him sloppy," Dani said, yanked her Glock from her holster and checked the clip. She pulled her Sigma from the bag over her shoulder and likewise checked that weapon. She jammed that one into her front waistband and covered it with the loose folds of her shirt.

"He'll know there are two of us," Mitch reminded her.

"I'll make it seem like I'm waiting for you." She detailed her plan, and while Mitch wasn't in love with using her as bait, the plan made perfect sense.

They hurried down the narrow street and kept to the tight alleys between the rows of homes along the winding streets of Trastevere. A cold sweat broke out along his body as he remembered the last time he had made a similar journey. One that had nearly cost him his life.

At the mouth of one side street, they paused.

Time to separate.

Dani glanced at him and concern flooded her face. "You

okay?" She laid her hand on his jaw, and he realized how cold and clammy his skin was at the warmth of her touch.

He couldn't admit he was afraid. More afraid than he'd ever been before on the hundreds of missions he had undertaken as an Army Ranger and then as a Lazlo operative.

"Just be careful out there," he said, and before she could protest, bent and kissed her.

To his surprise, she answered his kiss, pressing herself against him before she turned and raced off in the direction of the hotel.

Muttering a curse, he sped in the opposite direction to take his place in their trap.

Chapter 13

Dani knew what she looked like in her black miniskirt, low-cut blouse and stiletto-heeled knee-high black boots. So she played it up, swinging her hips and smiling at the men she passed along the street leading to the hotel. The fake black hair swayed with her attention-getting stride, and she tossed her head back, playing the coquette as she turned onto the block for the hotel.

She tuned in every sense to the world around her, looking for anyone with a build like that of the killer. Not much to go on and not much to see on the relatively quiet block.

Reaching the end of the building before the hotel, she opted to wait there. The courtyard beyond might be difficult to escape if someone boxed her in. She picked up her leg, exposing quite a bit of skin as she placed one foot up against the rough stone wall and leaned back against it, her one hand tucked behind her and on the grip of her Glock.

She waited, the seconds seeming like hours. Someone came out of the courtyard area. A tall, thin man dressed all in black and carrying a book in his hands. He seemed to be reading, but Dani wasn't about to take any chances.

She tightened her hand on the grip of the gun, but the man picked up his head then, revealing the strip of white at his collar. Knowing it could still be a ploy and that the killer could have been wearing body armor or something else that would have made him appear more muscular, she smiled sexily at the priest.

He seemed genuinely embarrassed and hurried on, head buried more securely in the book.

As she watched him walk away, she heard the purr of an expensive engine a moment before the first pop of gunfire.

Beside her, bits of stone flew off the walls as the bullets traced a path in her direction.

She dropped to the ground behind the cover of the cars parked there and then jumped up in time to see Mitch stepping out from the opposite side of the street. He had grabbed a thick length of wood from somewhere and swung it at the shooter, who was riding a costly Ducati and firing at her with an Uzi.

Home run, Dani thought as the man went flying back and the Uzi flew out of his hand. The Ducati roared ahead a few feet before careening into a few parked cars.

Mitch stood there, gun trained on the helmeted assassin, who was slowly getting to his feet.

"Get down," Mitch commanded, but the man seemed hell-bent on ignoring him.

Dani fixed her gun on him as well, but then a car screeched out of a spot barely five yards away and came straight at Mitch. Without a second's thought, she launched herself at him, heedless of her own safety. She connected with him solidly, driving him away from the center of the road and the path of the car.

They landed hard on the cobblestoned street, a tangle of arms and legs. By the time they scrambled to their feet, their assailant had climbed into the car, which sped away, burning rubber.

Dani raised her gun and fired off a round of shots as did Mitch, but they only managed to crack the back windshield.

The noise brought people from their homes and the hotel. A siren sounded, growing louder the longer they stood there.

Looking up the street, she noticed the Ducati lying just up the block. "Let's go," she said, but as she took a step, pain lanced up her left side. Debilitating pain that nearly drove her to her knees.

Mitch was suddenly there, arm around her waist, offering support. "Are you hit?" he asked as he half carried her toward the motorcycle.

"Don't think so," she said, although it hurt to breathe. She managed to look down, but didn't see any blood and as Mitch released her to pick up the motorcycle, she staggered against a parked car and grabbed at her side. The side that had been bothering her since the training session in Paris.

"Can you get on?" Mitch asked, even as he was swinging a leg over the motorcycle and holding out his hand.

She grabbed hold and slipped onto the back of the bike. Once she was settled, she wrapped her arms around him and he said, "Where to?"

"Tarquinia."

The man spat up blood as he slumped forward in the passenger seat beside Troy. Too much? Troy wondered when the paid assassin groaned and finally forced himself upright.

"Broke a damn rib thanks to your stupid plan," the man said, ripping the black ski mask from his face and tossing it to the floor.

"Can you finish the job?" Troy asked, expertly steering the car around one corner and dragging another complaint from his companion as the sharp movement jostled him. When he had righted the car, his companion gripped his side and with a shaky breath said, "Of course not, you ignorant ass. Think my lung's punctured."

"That's what I thought."

Troy pulled over into the driveway behind a small store.

"What are you doing?" The man coughed again, his breath rasping roughly in his chest before he straightened in his seat once more. Pink spittle stained his lips. His face was pale.

"Finishing this," Troy said as he pulled out his gun.

The injured assassin's eyes opened wide with surprise, but Troy fired before the man could reach for his own gun. A clean shot straight in the middle of his forehead.

Afterward, he walked away from the car , but stopped a few feet away as he retched at the thought of what he had just done. He'd had no choice in this business. It was kill or be killed.

His mother might not think that he could handle jobs such as this, but he knew differently. He was going to put an end to this nasty business with the Lazlo Group, even if it meant bringing down the top man himself.

They stopped to retrieve the bags they had hidden on their way back from Lazlo headquarters, knowing they would be too bulky during a fight. Dani didn't move from the bike as she ripped off the black wig, exposing the longer strands of her hair. Every movement seemed to pain her, but Mitch knew she wouldn't like to be babied.

He handed her black bag to her, but she could only get the strap over one shoulder, clearly favoring her left side. Aware that he couldn't wear his own knapsack with her riding behind him, he said, "On second thought, let me have your bag."

"I can handle—"

"We don't have time to argue, Dani. Just give me the bag," he said and although she glared at him, she handed it to him.

He managed to tie together the straps of both their bags and hang them over the gas tank as if they were *saddlebags*. Then he squeezed on before her again and as he did so, Dani provided instructions for getting on the *autostrada*.

He didn't ask why Tarquinia. He suspected she had her reasons, and anger filled him that she hadn't told him earlier. That anger was tempered by the small sounds of her pain as they drove along. Each bump and jolt registered with him as it did with her. Her hands would tighten at his sides or he would hear her muffled moan against his back.

They had been traveling nearly forty-five minutes along the *autostrada* when he noticed the first signs announcing their imminent arrival in Tarquinia. But even if they hadn't reached their destination, he would have stopped, as Dani's grasp on him had begun to get tenuous.

He worried about her condition and how badly she was injured.

A quick inspection in the alley where they had paused to retrieve their bags hadn't revealed any gunshot injuries other than a few cuts and scratches on her face from the stone blown off the wall beside her.

He took the first exit, but instead of heading toward town, he detoured away to the open fields nearby, which eventually led to a wooded area not far from a large farmhouse up on a nearby hill. He drove the Ducati up the road leading to the farmhouse, but then slowed and turned the motorcycle into a small clearing in the woods.

As before, each rough bump elicited a complaint from Dani.

When he finally killed the engine and rolled the bike to a stop, Dani's hands dropped from his sides.

He looked over his shoulder at her. Her face was drawn and pale. She leaned her hand on his shoulder heavily as she swung her leg over the bike and stood.

"I need to sit," she said and stumbled back a few steps to the base of a large pine tree. Leaning back against it, she slowly sank down, one arm wrapped around her side.

Mitch walked over and kneeled in front of her. "What's wrong?"

"Side," she said, her breath choppy. "Pulled something."

"Lie down. Let me see."

He helped her onto the bed of pine needles beneath the tree, but even that change of position brought her discomfort. She was breathing shallowly, unable to draw a really deep breath and he gently urged her to relax.

"Easy, Dani. Slow breaths before you hyperventilate."

She closed her eyes and focused. Slowly her breaths lengthened, although he could see that each one pained her. He eased up the loose folds of her shirt, exposing the Sigma still tucked into the waistband of her short skirt. He removed it, and that she didn't protest was a testament to her distress.

Raising the shirt to just beneath her bra, he immediately noticed the beginnings of a bruise along the side of her ribs. He softly ran his hand there. "Is this where it hurts?"

She shook her head and opened her eyes. "That's from

when I hit you. You're kind of hard," she teased, clearly trying to ease his disquiet.

"Show me, then," he said and she moved her hand to right above the middle of her rib cage.

"Here," she said, and he ran his hand and pressed on a rib. When she didn't respond, he moved to the intercostal muscle between her ribs and pressed.

Her body jumped and she moaned at the pressure on that point. "That's it."

"Rib muscle pull. We need to immobilize it, but it'll still hurt."

"I can deal," she said and rolled to her uninjured side to sit up. He could see that the movement cost her.

Beads of sweat dotted her upper lip, and the color drained from her face.

"Maybe we should—"

"No. We need to finish this mission no matter what," Dani replied adamantly.

He wasn't going to argue with her, but he wasn't sure he agreed about finishing the mission. However, he wasn't the one to make that call.

He handed her Sigma back to her and stood. "I'm going to reconnoiter. Get clothes and food. Something to bind your ribs. Don't go anywhere."

"As if I could," she teased once more, dragging a reluctant smile from him.

"I'll be back," he said and started to walk away, but Dani called to him and he stopped.

"Don't contact Lazlo, Mitch. We need to stay deep cover until we know how to safely communicate."

He glanced at the PDA on his hip, still powered up and

possibly broadcasting their signal to the world. He shut it off, pulled it from his belt and tossed it to Dani.

"In case of an emergency," he said, hoping he wouldn't regret making the decision to go it alone.

Chapter 14

The late afternoon sun was bright overhead, filtering through the wispy branches of the pines above down into the small clearing, warming her. The ride on the back of the motorcycle had been a little chilly, even with the August heat.

Dani eyeballed the branches overhead as well as the underbrush surrounding her—they would provide sufficient cover against anyone coming up the road or searching for them from the air.

Picking up Mitch's PDA, she wondered if someone had gotten a fix on them before he had shut it off. *Which* someone was what bothered her. Presumably only Lazlo and his people were aware of their mission and location. Which of them had tipped off SNAKE?

It would be safest to avoid using any of their communication devices, including their satellite computer hookups, until they could disguise their location. In the meantime, she guessed that they were no more than an hour away from the country villa of Olivia Alegria. Although she wanted to get there sooner rather than later, she was sure she wasn't up to it today.

The soreness in her side had receded to a dull persistent ache, but movement brought a knifelike stabbing pain. Anything faster than a slow walk seemed out of the question right now since she couldn't really catch a deep breath.

Mitch had questioned her about whether she could continue the mission, and while she had initially indicated that they had to finish the operation no matter what, the time spent waiting for him had her wondering if it was fair for her to do so. She had promised to watch Mitch's back, and in her current condition, she'd be more of a hindrance than a help.

A soft footfall alerted her to a presence nearby.

She picked up her Sigma and pointed it in the general direction of the sound, but a minute later, Mitch came out of the woods, carrying a bleached white sheet that he had bundled around some items.

He smiled and kneeled at her side. "Got a few things and found somewhere we can spend the night."

Placing the sheet on the ground, he opened it to reveal bottled water, another sheet, some clothes and a bottle of pain medication. He handed her the bottled water and medication. "Take those. I'm going to shred this sheet so we can wrap your ribs."

The ibuprofen said to take one or two. She spilled out four into her hand and downed them with the water while Mitch ripped the sheet lengthwise, creating a nice wide and fairly long bandage for her ribs. First she had to get her shirt off.

Luckily the flexible fabric allowed her to slip her arm out one side first, then the other. With her good arm, she pulled it over her head, then leaned back against the trunk of the pine tree, sweating from the minor exertion.

Mitch had wound up the makeshift bandage and now he showed it to her. "I need you to stand and exhale as far as you can. We need to give those ribs some support."

He rose, held out his hand and she took it and slowly came to her feet. She placed her hands on his shoulders to keep her arms out of the way, exhaled until the first twinge came, then pressed just a little more and finally held her breath.

Mitch worked quickly, wrapping the soft fabric of the sheet around her ribs over and over. As he neared the end of the wrap, he tore the sheet in half and, reversing the direction of one of the strips, tied off the wrap in front.

She inhaled and as her inhalation deepened, the wrap did what it was supposed to, taking some of the burden from her intercostal muscles and lessening the pain. "It's better. Thanks."

He dropped his hands to her waist. "No need to thank me. If anything, I should be thanking you."

She shook her head, slightly confused. "Why?"

"For everything from the lack of safe in the safe house and PDA connection to you knocking me out of the way of that car. That couldn't have helped your ribs."

"I didn't think we were keeping score." She turned her back to him and cautiously bent to pick up the clothes he had pilfered for her use. The plain cotton blouse would be easy to put on as would the roomy jeans. The shoes he had found were a trifle large, but the thick socks would make up for it.

Unzipping the boots, she tossed them on top of the shirt she had discarded earlier. The miniskirt joined the pile.

When she faced Mitch once again, he was standing there, arms across his chest. His face unreadable.

"The farmhouse has a small outbuilding that looks like it

was used to store old equipment. I scrounged up some supplies and set up camp there."

"What about whoever's living in the farmhouse?" she asked, bending to toss all her belongings except her Glock and Sigma onto the other sheet Mitch had brought with him. Picking up the edges, she twisted the top to create a makeshift bag.

"They seem to be gone for now. It is August, so maybe they're on vacation. The outbuilding has a view of the main house, though, so we'll be able to see any activity."

He motioned in the direction of the farmhouse. "I'll walk the bike. We'll need it to go to…"

He rolled his index finger around, gesturing for her to fill in the blank, but instead she said, "Let's get settled. Then we can decide what to do."

Mitch let out a harsh laugh. "So it's a 'we' now."

"It was always a 'we', Mitch." She put her hands on her hips, trying for as defiant a pose as she could without straining her ribs.

"Didn't sound like a 'we' when you told me to head to wherever it is that we are," he said, matching her pose, arms akimbo. His muscles tensed.

"You're right and I apologize."

He was clearly taken aback. "You apologize?"

"I wanted to tell you tonight so we could decide, but it didn't happen. So, we're here in Tarquinia because it's close to the country villa of Olivia Alegria." She started to walk and Mitch quickly retrieved the bike and followed behind her.

"Alegria? Name doesn't mean a thing," he said as he trudged along.

"Typical American. She's the widow of Sergio Alegria, one of the world's best known footballers."

"Foot…oh, soccer. Not my thing," he admitted, but then

immediately added. "What does Alegria have to do with our assignment?"

She stopped and faced him, because any kind of twisting brought immediate pain even with the rib wrap. "I think SNAKE assassinated him a year ago."

The outbuilding Mitch had located was solidly built with windows facing the farmhouse, providing not only a good view but wonderful ventilation. Inside the small stone structure, there were four stalls, three of which were filled with harnesses and other tack, spare parts and smaller farm machines. In the central area, where Mitch wheeled the Ducati, sat an older Fiat Spider. Whether or not it was functional was anyone's guess since it looked like it hadn't been driven in some time.

In the one free space closest to the windows facing the farmhouse, sweet-smelling hay filled a stall and sloped gently into one corner. Mitch had placed a comforter over the hay, where they could rest. Daylight waned and a rusty battery-powered lantern waited at the entrance of the stall.

A wedge of cheese, ripe peaches, a loaf of bread and a wine bottle that Mitch apparently raided from the empty farmhouse held a place of honor in the middle of the comforter.

"Looks great," she said. As she neared the edge of the thick bedspread, she toed off the sneakers, walked onto the fabric and made herself comfortable. Surprisingly so, she thought, since the slope of the hay took a great deal of pressure off her ribs.

"Feels even better," she said with a sigh, earning a smile from Mitch.

"Hopefully that makes us even."

Irritation flared within her. "Again, not keeping score. We're partners. We're—"

"A 'we'. I get it. Let's chow down before it gets too dark."

He positioned himself next to her but bent forward and with the rather substantial knife he took from a sheath on his belt, whacked off a few pieces of bread from the loaf. Then he sliced off some of the cheese, put it on the bread and handed her a piece.

For himself, he snagged the bottle of wine, yanked off the cork and took a sip. He grimaced. "It's almost fruit juice, which I guess is good."

Dani bit into the bread and cheese, her appetite revived now that the discomfort in her side seemed under control. The sharp cheese and yeasty semolina bread were heaven. Or maybe she was just that hungry.

Mitch held out the wine bottle to her. "Sorry. No glasses."

Grabbing the bottle from him, she took a swig and watched as he wolfed down a big hunk of bread and cheese, and then cut some more.

The wine was much like he had said. So new that it was close to grape juice due to the lack of fermenting. After another sip, she passed the bottle back to him.

They ate some more. Drank some more. Mitch handed her a peach and she took a bite. The juices ran down her mouth and the fruit was sweet. She moaned at the lushness of the flavor.

"It doesn't get any better than this," she said. She licked her lips and was about to wipe away the juices with her hand when Mitch said, "Let me."

He bent toward her, licked away the juices from the edges of her lips, then opened his mouth on hers, kissing her until she clung to him. But she had to hang on to sanity as well, and in between kisses, she said, "I thought last night was all about getting over this need."

He chuckled but kept on kissing her, even as he said, "It was."

She applied gentle pressure on his shoulders, urging him to stop for a moment. "So what's this?"

Mitch smiled, but it was tinged with sadness. "This is my taking advantage of our vulnerable emotional state."

Our, Dani thought. At least it was mutual. "An honest assessment of the situation," she said, knowing they had to rein in those runaway emotions because to surrender to them might only bring untold pain at the end of this mission.

With a nod, Mitch sat up, reached for the bottle of wine and took another slug. He held it out to her, but she shook her head. Leaning on her good side, she pushed off the hay and sat up against the wooden slats of the stall. The movement brought one twinge through her ribs, but not as much pain as before. The wrap, medicine and wine had probably assisted in dulling the ache.

"We need to consider what to do next."

Mitch shrugged, picked up a peach and bit into it, but as his gaze met hers, he clearly wished he was biting into something else. In response, her nipples tightened beneath the cotton of her shirt.

"You're Answer Girl. You think Alegria's death wasn't an accident, so tell me why."

Dani ran through the information she had gotten from the files the night before. He listened carefully, although the way he was eating that damned peach proved distracting time and again. She was grateful when he finished, took another slug of the wine and offered up what was left.

She grabbed the bottle and polished off the last sip. Then, she returned to her report. "I want to question Olivia Alegria about her suspicions regarding the foundation and about Breckenridge."

"Seems strange that at every turn, Breckenridge's name keeps popping up," Mitch agreed. He grabbed his knapsack, removed his computer and slipped the modem card from its slot.

As she watched him remove it, Mitch explained. "You were right about not using the PDA. Once we establish any kind of connection to a cellular service, they could triangulate our position."

"So how will you connect—"

"The farmhouse has a wireless router. Hopefully unsecured. I'm going to spoof the IP address and other identifying details on this laptop and try to get a message off to Lucia." His fingers flew over the keys as he spoke.

"Sounds like you know what you're doing," she said, realizing that she wanted to know more about the man that he was and what he could do.

With another shrug of those broad muscular shoulders, he said, "I have a master's in computer science, and communications was one of my specialties as a Ranger."

She knew that he'd been an Army Ranger, like the one her sister Lizzy Bee had married—Aidan Spaulding, Mitch's best friend and former partner. "Is that how you met Aidan?" she asked, eager to know more about both men.

He didn't look up or stop typing as he said, "We met at boot camp. Had a lot in common."

"Like what?" She had seen his file, but wanted Mitch's take on the things that were important to him,

"We were both military brats and had spent most of our lives moving from one assignment to another," he said, shooting her a glance as he worked. "Much like I imagine you did as the Sparrow."

Her life as the Sparrow had been a series of adventures in more countries than she cared to count. "I got around, but I had a stable home in Leonia. At least, I did before my parents were murdered."

Mitch detected the wistfulness in her voice and the distress. It dragged him from the work he had been trying to do and he stopped in the middle of his programming, examined her in the fading light. "You miss that other life."

Even in the growing darkness, the glint of unshed tears in her eyes couldn't be missed. Nor could the slight huskiness in her voice as she answered, "It was a wonderful life. Sometimes I wish…"

At her hesitation, he leaned closer to examine her face and asked, "What do you wish?"

She shrugged. "It's a silly wish."

"What is it?" he pressed, wanting more than just her body. Wanting to understand what she kept bottled up in her heart.

"That it could be as simple as it was before my parents died. That I could go home again."

He recalled the year of their involvement. Remembered the happiness they had shared, and the hopes. Normal hopes like those that most people had. Dreams of making a home. Having children. Growing old together.

Things he had never thought possible for himself until he'd met Dani. Her words confirmed to him that she had wanted the same things.

"Doesn't sound so silly to me. Do you know what I wish for?"

He waited for her to say more, but when she didn't, he offered, "I was an Army brat. Didn't have anywhere I could really call home, but sometimes I wish I could find a place."

Her head whipped in his direction. "Do you?"

He shrugged, afraid of revealing too much. "Sometimes. I heard from Lazlo how happy Aidan is with Elizabeth. It made me think that if my old Army buddy could do it…"

He didn't need to finish. She understood, but she clearly didn't want to take the discussion further. Instead, she pointed to his laptop. "Are you having any luck in connecting?"

He told himself it was better that they got back to work. There were already too many distractions jeopardizing this assignment. "It'll take me some time to make sure I don't give away our location. Why don't you lie down and get some rest until then."

"Sure." She carefully eased back onto the bed of hay and closed her eyes.

He returned to work and could tell from her breathing when she finally slipped off to sleep.

He paused then and examined her as she rested. Welcome color had returned to her face and she seemed to be moving better, but he remained conscious of the fact she wasn't one hundred percent. On an operation like this one, that could risk both their lives.

Returning to the programming, he considered asking Lazlo to call off the assignment, but he owed the other man a great deal and couldn't leave him in a lurch. Especially not when the lives of other agents might be in jeopardy. He could continue alone, but suspected Dani would have none of that.

As he finished the coding that would hide their location and the source of their communications, he engaged the basic wireless card in the laptop. A few seconds later, the icon on the system tray acknowledged that a wireless signal was available. A weak one, but that would have to do for now.

He grinned as he opened the connections and realized that the router back up at the farmhouse was unsecured, as he had suspected.

"You're smiling," Dani said sleepily and rubbed a hand across her face before sitting up.

Full night had fallen, and the glow from the laptop provided the sole illumination in the stall. "We've got a connection. I'm going to e-mail Lucia at one of her safe accounts."

Dani arched an eyebrow, obviously dubious of his claim. "Well, as safe as safe can be right now. Tomorrow we buy some prepaid cell phones and try to make contact."

"Sounds like a plan, only, could we keep Alegria's name out of this for now?"

He nodded, drafting a quick e-mail to Lucia.

Will contact tomorrow. Provide secure number. Little Bird's wings have been bruised.

He paused, his earlier hesitation rising up. He knew that the right words from him could result in the termination of their assignment. Glancing upward, he realized Dani watched him intently. Did she sense his indecision?

With a deep breath, he plowed on, finishing the message in the only way he suspected would sit right with the woman sitting just a few feet away.

However, Little Bird can still fly. Mission is a go.

Chapter 15

Troy sauntered into his mother's office, guilt still gnawing at him about how he had dealt with their hired gun and annoyed that the two Lazlo agents had eluded him. Still, his mother seemed to have a solid connection to someone who could help tidy up those loose ends so he had seen no sense in lingering in Rome.

She sat at the ornate eighteenth century rococo desk, flipping through some papers on her desk. She didn't look up as he entered but kept examining the file in her hands.

"*Avez-vous des nouvelles?*" he asked, wanting her to remain unaware of his participation in the assignment until he had truly proven himself.

She finally deigned to look up at him. "News? Actually, I received an e-mail advising that Kruger and another Lazlo operative were dead. My inside source confirmed it, but also advised that we've got two Lazlo agents on the loose."

With a negligent shrug, he took a seat before his mother, crossed his legs and straightened the pleat on his pants. "We will deal with it, Maman."

His mother's gaze narrowed as she considered him. Something about him apparently worried her. "You don't seem surprised by my report nor all that nervous about the agents."

He gave another casual shrug and smiled confidently. "You always accomplish what you want. Should this assignment be any different?"

He could see that she wanted to slap that smugness from his face. Cassandra held back, however, seemingly sure that she had a better way to strike down his confidence.

"Only if finally putting the Sparrow in her grave is of importance."

He bolted forward in his chair. "What did you say?"

"My source tells me that the Sparrow is alive and working for Lazlo on this mission."

"That can't be," he said, but even as the words left his mouth, he was trying to recall what he had seen in Rome.

"Is there something I should know, *mon fils?*"

Troy settled back into the comfort of the leather chair and crossed his legs once again, attempting to strike a relaxed pose when he was anything but. In his mind he replayed the quick glimpse of the female Lazlo operative—the long, luscious legs visible beneath the short hem of her miniskirt. The voluptuous but petite body and short black hair, glossy in the Rome sun.

Maybe too glossy he considered now, thinking that it might have been a wig.

He hadn't gotten a good look at her face. He had been too busy keeping an eye on their hired gun and the man who had challenged him as he fired on the woman in the miniskirt.

"Troy?" his mother pressed at his silence.

"Do you trust your source?" he asked, unwilling to believe that the Sparrow had somehow survived being shot by Donovan. All reports at the time had been to the contrary.

"My source is impeccable."

Even impeccable sources could sometimes be wrong. "There's one sure way to—"

"Been there, done that, *mon cheri*," his mother said and waved her hand with a flourish.

"You grabbed her twin sister?" Troy asked, chagrined that his mother had beat him to the punch yet again.

"She's disappeared along with her new husband. Rumors have them going on a much delayed honeymoon trip."

Their sudden absence only served to confirm his mother's earlier assertion. "So the Sparrow's alive. Interesting, but not fatal—except to her," he said.

Cassandra leaned forward, not amused by his comment. "Don't underestimate her. She fooled us and most of the world for years."

Troy stood and pulled on his suit jacket to straighten the shoulders. "Second time's a charm, Mother. Let me—"

"No, *mon fils. Pas vous*. I paid well to have the Lazlo agents eliminated and that job hasn't been finished. I'll make sure that it is," she said and seemed unprepared for his ready acquiescence.

"*Naturellement*. I'm sure your hired gun is already on their trail," he said, but as she watched him go, he knew she was worried. It was a mother's lot in life to worry, after all.

Mitch finished typing and immediately turned on the battery-powered lantern, setting it to the lowest level. Then he shut down the computer. "Conserving power. Lucia won't e-mail back until she's sure she's got a completely clean connection."

With a nod, Dani said, "Let's go over those agents we identified the other night."

Mitch handed her bag to her. He brought over the lantern and sat close beside her while she removed the papers, setting aside those of the agents with whom she had some acquaintance—much as she had done the night before.

He pointed to them. "Those are—"

"People I know to some extent."

"Which makes them free from scrutiny?" he challenged, although it lacked any sting.

"No, just lower on the list than this man," she said and pulled out the information she had cobbled together on Williams.

"The nancy boy again. He fits Kruger's description. Do you find him that attractive?" He took the papers from her hand and shot her a half glance while going through the papers.

"If you're into men who like to primp and preen," she said deadpan, although she knew her comment would strike home with Mitch and his usual sartorial habits.

Mitch just grunted and focused his attention on Williams's financial records, one of the more important pieces of information she had been able to collect from a private credit firm database to which she still had access. He let out a low whistle. "Man spends loads of money. Pricey flat and auto. Expensive clothes and equally extravagant dining habits."

"More than someone at his pay grade would earn," Dani advised, well familiar with the salary since she had at one time been at a similar grade.

"Old money perhaps?" Mitch turned back to Williams's bio, read through it slowly before looking up at her. "Now there's a familiar name again."

"Williams's dad used to be partners with Barrett Jenkins."

"Too much coincidence, but we're going to need more than this to take to the authorities," Mitch said.

Dani took back the pages, shuffled through them once again but could find nothing else that was useful. "We'll need to do more digging. Connect all the extra money that Williams has to Jenkins as well as figure out how Breckenridge fits into this puzzle."

Bending his head, Mitch examined her intently. "You think Breckenridge has some connection to this?"

Dani counted down each point on a finger. "Jenkins has been counsel to Breckenridge for some time. Breckenridge received a check from the foundation that Lazlo was asked to investigate. The agent on that investigation is now dead."

"Circumstantial at best. Plus we have no proof of any wrongdoing on the part of any of these three men."

She glanced down at Williams in the dim light cast by the lantern. Kruger was likely dead, so it was only their best guess that Williams had been the agent with whom Kruger had spoken. Again she wondered why the agent had come into the room after all the other agents had left, but then it occurred to her.

Whipping out the papers once again, she reread his bio and assignment details. Pointing at one section, she said to Mitch, "Williams has reported to several old-timers at SIS on various assignments. He could have noticed their disdain for the Lazlo Group."

"And if he heard that Kruger had some connection to a Lazlo Group mission, he might have taken it upon himself to scope it out on behalf of his superiors," Mitch said, connecting the dots.

Unfortunately, connecting those dots created a totally different picture than the one involving Jenkins and Breckenridge. "We're back to square one, aren't we?" she said and leaned back against the wooden partition of the stall.

"Maybe our conversation with Olivia Alegria will shed some more light on things. Why don't you get some rest?"

Dani shook her head. "Wide awake after that nap. Why don't you take the first shift? I want to do a little more digging into all our suspects."

Mitch handed her his laptop. "Use this. There's a spare battery in my knapsack."

She took his computer, and Mitch sacked out on the comforter-covered hay, his back to her and away from the low light of the lantern.

Dani immediately powered up the PC and opted to search out more information on Breckenridge and Jenkins. As public figures, they would appear on the various news services and private databases to which she had access, an easier search than SIS records. Those would have to wait until Lucia could provide secure communications once more.

Using various Internet search engines, she scoured through an assortment of news articles, trying to glean any information she could that would hint at some kind of improper activity on the part of either Jenkins or Breckenridge. What she got was a load of connections to various organizations that had made substantial contributions to Breckenridge's political campaign chest over the years. Included in that list was an organization that prided itself as a government watchdog on cases that included wrongful imprisonment, which could explain Jenkins's representation of Kruger.

A few hours passed and the low-battery warning came on the laptop. Setting the computer aside, she reached for Mitch's knapsack and as she pulled it toward her, his passport folder fell out of the front pocket. When it landed on the comforter, some of the contents spilled out and as she gathered them up, she noted the picture of Mitch and her, snapped during one of his trips to visit her in Rome.

Such happier times, she thought, running her finger across their smiling faces. He had his arms wrapped around her shoulders and one of her one hands rested on his where they twined around her. She remembered when the picture had been taken by a tourist on one of their walks through Rome.

As she eased the photo back into the leather folder along with the other papers, she realized how worn the edges of the photo were, as if it had been well-handled. Had he looked at it often in the three long years since they had last seen each other in that back alley with his life's blood spilling all over her hands?

Shouldn't he have let you know he wasn't dead? her inner demon reminded, trying to drive away the nostalgia sure to confuse her even more about her feelings for Mitch.

Feelings for Mitch, she thought. The last thing they needed on this mission was anything else that would cause problems. They had enough of those as it was, and she reminded herself that the feelings for him that were slowly coming back had to be contained.

Returning the folder to the front pouch of the knapsack, she dug her hand inside, retrieved the battery and got back to work, but as she glanced over the edge of the display to Mitch's broad back as he slept, she couldn't help wondering what he had been feeling for those three long years. Whether he had been as lonely as she had been.

She forced herself to return to work, much as she had after her parents had died. Back then the work had not only made it easier to forget their loss, it had provided the money that she and her sister Lizzy Bee had needed to survive.

Lizzy Bee, she thought with a pang of loneliness. How she wished she had her sister to speak with. To tell about all the conflicting emotions roiling within her, but she couldn't speak with Lizzy Bee until this mission was completed.

Which provided added incentive to get back to work. Once the assignment was over, she would not only be able to see her sister, she'd be able to get on with her life and so would Mitch.

She ignored the annoying voice in her head that asked whether her new life would be with or without him.

Chapter 16

After his mother's stunning pronouncement, sleep eluded Troy. If his mother's sources were correct and the Sparrow still lived, he needed to track her down and eliminate her.

He had sped off with Cassandra's hired gun before getting a fix on the Lazlo operatives. He'd had to take care of the assassin, and by then the trail had been cold. The Ducati they had probably taken could have gone in a number of different directions, but if it were up to him, he'd head for the *autostrada* and try to put as much distance as possible between himself and their failed mission.

With Kruger dead, there had likely been little reason for the Sparrow and her hulking assistant to stay in Rome. But to be more certain of that, he had to better familiarize himself with the Sparrow.

He lay in bed, laptop on his legs and connected to the Dumont network. His mother had kept a detailed file on the world-renowned assassin, tracking many of her more well-known cases before inviting her to join their organization. That the Sparrow had managed to deceive them had infuriated his mother, which was why Cassandra had set up Silas Donovan to kill her.

Somehow she had survived the shooting. Troy had no doubt the Lazlo Group had some hand in that and in keeping her out of jail for her role in helping assassinate the young prince of Silvershire.

He read through the file, making mental notes of her various skills and the many places she had carried out her assignments. The Sparrow had been all over the world but had repeatedly struck at targets in Europe. The file his mother had somehow obtained from SIS detailed that she spoke several languages. It also had one of those passport-style photos of the Sparrow, real name Danielle Moore.

Not even the poor photography could hide that she was attractive. He recalled the sight of her as she leaned against the building. The long legs and toned body. The full breasts hugged by the tight shirt she wore.

The Sparrow was known for being plain, but she had been anything but when he had seen her—a decided change in MO, possibly because of her new assignment as a Lazlo Group operative. The file indicated her hair was brown, but even from the picture he could tell her hair was more auburn than anything.

The short black hair she had worn in Rome had been a wig, much as he had suspected.

Saving the file to his laptop, he turned his attention to figuring out where they might have gone and whether it had anything to do with what Kruger had told them.

There was one possible way to know. Turning to the traffic

system for the *autostrada*, he channeled through the various web cam locations that provided the public with views of the current traffic situation on the public highways. If they were still on the road, he might be able to spot the distinctive Ducati.

After surfing for some time, he saw nothing on the mostly quiet thoroughfares which meant that they could have pulled off for the night. But they might have been captured by the cameras earlier. He picked up the phone and dialed the Dumont computer guru.

When the man answered, he was groggy with sleep and as Troy glanced at his watch, he realized that it was well past midnight. No matter. Come the morning, he intended to carry out the instructions his mother had left on the cell phone tucked into his pocket. She had called the dead assassin after Troy had exited the room and left the command that the two Lazlo agents be killed.

Troy was going to be the one who tracked down the Sparrow and eliminated her and her friend before they could cause any more problems. Maybe for good measure, he would add the elusive Corbett Lazlo to the list and show his mother once and for all that he was capable of helping her run their family business.

Mitch woke just after two in the morning, feeling refreshed after the few hours of sleep.

Dani had been sitting against the partition, eyes half-closed and her Sigma resting in one hand on her lap. He knew better than to assume she wasn't alert enough to react to any challenge.

Apparently she sensed the change in his breathing rhythm. Her eyes opened and she shot him a tired smile. "Ready to take watch?"

He nodded and they switched positions, Dani making herself comfortable in the indent created in the hay by his bigger body. As she lay down, he noticed she still favored her injured side and winced when she settled on her left side, facing him. That was her sleeping side, he remembered from the many times they had shared a bed.

"You okay?" he questioned, still concerned about Dani's state of preparedness.

"Much better. Don't worry about me, worry about the mission."

He wanted to say that it was one and the same, but that would only trigger an argument and Dani needed to rest. Grabbing his laptop, he tried to power it up, but it wouldn't turn on. Dani's investigations had drained it dry, and her laptop was a different make with a different battery. He didn't want to worry about reprogramming her computer to provide the needed security.

He picked up the lantern, rose and searched the walls of the outbuilding, but there wasn't a plug in sight. By the time he returned to Dani's side, the deep and regular cadence of her breathing signaled that she slept. As he went to sit, the light from the lantern illuminated the chrome bumper of the Fiat Spider sitting in the center of the outbuilding, partially covered by some tarps.

They would need a ride to the Alegria estate, and the Ducati would be too obvious. Plus, they needed to consider a change in appearance. If their location had been compromised, it was highly possible their identities had been revealed as well. He vaguely recalled what had looked like a box of hair dye in the farmhouse medicine cabinet when he had been foraging through there for some pain meds for Dani.

At the door of the outbuilding, he checked for any signs

that the farmhouse inhabitants had returned. Nothing. Sneaking out, he crept up to the house and once again inspected it for signs of life. No car sat in the drive and all the lights were still out. Maybe the homeowners were away as he had suspected earlier.

He swung around to the back door and quickly jimmied the lock with his credit card again. Entering, he waited to see if any noise indicated that someone was home. Like earlier in the day, no sound came. He immediately went upstairs to the master bathroom. The medicine chest held a box of blond hair dye.

He grabbed the box. Scouring the master bedroom closet, he found a man's lightweight cotton sweater. It would come in handy in hiding the tattoo on his arm, which might clue in someone to his real identity.

On his way out, he stopped to search the kitchen drawers for one last thing—a pair of scissors. Going blond would certainly help disguise them, but a quick cut of Dani's hair would seal the deal.

Before he returned to the outbuilding, he grabbed some more food from their fridge and placed what he thought were enough euros to compensate the family for his thievery on the kitchen counter.

Dani was still out when he made his way back. Placing his booty on the comforter, he turned his attention to the Fiat, removing the tarp to check out its general state.

The engine was only partially assembled, and a number of parts lay on a weathered oak table beside the automobile. Someone had clearly been restoring the older vehicle. Now it would be up to him to get it reassembled and working. He turned up the battery-powered lantern as high as he could and surprisingly it provided ample light in the small space close to the Fiat.

Working as quietly as he could so as to not wake Dani, he

carefully rebuilt the engine, checking each of the parts as he did so to make sure they seemed functional. It took hours and his back ached from hunching into the space to remount the various pieces onto the engine block.

He grew warm from his exertions and he pulled off his shirt and tossed it to the side as he worked. He had just finished tightening the screw on the last piece when Dani approached, pulling back the tumbled locks of her long hair and yawning the sleep from her system.

"Do you think it will work?"

He shrugged, snagged the keys from the work table and tossed them to her. "Give it a shot."

She slid behind the steering wheel and a moment later the car sputtered but didn't turn over.

Dani returned to stand by the front fender and motioned to the engine. "Did you check to see if the plugs were fouled?"

"Not yet. Want to help?" he said and was surprised when she said, "Yes."

She walked around the front of the car, grabbed a ratchet wrench, slipped on a deep socket and with a hip check to clear him out of the way, went to work on the spark plugs.

Her movements were efficient and sure as she disconnected the wires and used the wrench to remove the first spark plug. She held it up and said, "See. It's nasty. I'm assuming we don't have replacements."

Mitch shook his head. "Not anywhere that I can see."

She tossed him the spark plug. "Then take a wire brush to it while I get out the others."

He did as she instructed, cleaning the dirt and corrosion from the spark plug while she removed the rest. As he watched he said, "So is this something you learned at SIS?"

Her hands paused above one spark plug and she looked up

at him. "My Da. He had this old roadster he refused to part with. I'd help him work on it while my sister helped my mom with the cooking. Da taught me all about fixing cars."

"Do you still have it?" he asked, almost immediately regretting it as sadness played over her features.

"Lizzy has it in a garage not far from her restaurant. She keeps it running for me so I can drive it when I go home. It keeps me close to him somehow."

She yanked off another wire and tackled the removal of another spark plug as he set aside the one he had cleaned and began with another. "So I guess when we're done with this, you'll go home to Leonia?"

Dani didn't look up that time, but instead kept her attention trained on her task. Her voice was a little husky as she spoke. "I'm not sure. Leonia is the closest thing to home although I don't like spending a lot of time there."

"Why?"

This time she did give him a fleeting glance. "Makes me miss my Ma and Da too much."

He wondered whether she would ever get over their loss. Whether finding justice for them would help her find peace.

"And you?" she asked when he remained silent as he cleaned yet another plug.

"My dad and mom are in San Diego along with a brother and sister. I was never really close to them the way I was with Aidan."

"Who's married to Lizzy, so I guess home for him is Leonia as well," Dani said and took out the last spark plug, found another wire brush and started cleaning it.

"I guess." He wondered, whether if things had been different, Leonia might have become home for both of them. If together they could have built a life there.

Dani finished cleaning the plug and turned her attention

to checking the gap before reinstalling it. She did the same with each of the other plugs as he finished cleaning them, and when she was done, said, "Give it a try."

Mitch slipped behind the wheel and turned the ignition. The car sputtered again, for a longer time and with more power, but still stalled. From his spot in the driver's seat, he could see Dani playing with something under the hood—the air filter. A second later, she instructed, "Try again."

This time as he turned the key and the car sputtered, she fiddled with the carburetor and revved the engine. When she released the carburetor valve, the car did a rough little hiccup before settling into a regular and fairly smooth rhythm.

Smiling, he jumped from the seat and met Dani at the front of the car. "Great. So now there's only one more thing we need to do before we set out to get some prepaid phones."

"Really? What's that?" she asked, using a rag to wipe the grease from her hands.

He walked to the work table holding the remaining car parts, picked up the box of hair dye and the scissors and held them up. "Salon time," he said, but was unprepared for Dani's reaction.

"No way, no how." She stalked back to the sheet over the hay and began to gather what little things she had left, jerkily stuffing them into her leather knapsack.

He approached her, the box held in one hand. Scissors in the other. "We need new disguises. Cut and color will do the trick."

"And again I say no," she reiterated, sharply pulling closed the bindings on her bag.

"Don't be dense, Dani. It's—"

"Not necessary. The wig—"

"Is something they've seen already. We need to look totally different when we hit the streets again." He held up the box and reluctantly, Dani took it and read through the instructions.

"The color will wash out in eight to ten shampoos and the hair will grow back."

He wanted to say that gave her even less reason to object, but tears welled in her eyes. Stepping up to her, he cradled her cheek and swiped at the tear as it trailed down her cheek. "It *will* grow back."

With a soft sigh and half smile, she said, "Promise?"

"Promise."

Chapter 17

The silver of the mirror had tarnished and pitted, but it was still in good enough shape to show her the new do Mitch had styled for her.

Bowl-cut was too generous a description. Hack-job might be closer to reality. Her long locks now ended at mid-ear on the sides, but were longer in the back. Uneven, she realized as she ran her hand across the nape of her neck. Her entire head was bottle-blond now, and bangs swept across her forehead, accenting her high cheekbones and the green of her eyes.

"You okay?" Mitch asked and laid a hand on her shoulder.

His reflection met hers in the mirror, likewise bright-blond. As short as his hair had been, it hadn't taken much to cut back the longer strands up top before coloring what remained.

"I'm okay." How could she explain to him why losing the hair had been so traumatic. That for some reason her hair had been one of the few things left of the person she had been. Everything else was gone…well, gone for now.

Once they finished this mission, she would head home to her sister. Home to Leonia. Maybe there she could recover the woman she used to be.

"Ready to go?" He squeezed her shoulder gently and she nodded.

"Ready. Let me have the keys." She turned and held her hand out palm up.

"Just because you got it running—"

"Not just because. I've got more experience driving in Italy and know my way around better than you do." She wiggled her fingers and Mitch finally relented and dropped the keys into the palm of her hand.

Once on the road, she headed quickly into Tarquinia, where they located a cell phone store and purchased a trio of phones. Afterward, they headed to an Internet café. Mitch plugged in his laptop and texted the number for one of the cell phones to Lucia.

By the time they returned to the Fiat, that cell phone was ringing.

"Lucia?" Mitch leaned against the front fender of the sports car, and Dani leaned in to hear what Lucia reported.

"Mitch. How's Dani?" Lucia immediately asked.

"Dani is feeling better," he said, and Dani nodded her agreement with that assessment. "What happened in Rome?"

"We got our crew in after the fire was put out. Kruger and our agent were both shot once behind the ear, just like the last two Lazlo operatives. So were the security guards in the building."

"Our identities—"

"Assume they've been compromised just like your safe

house location." Mitch met Dani's gaze as Lucia said, "Someone knows the Sparrow is alive."

"Damn," Dani cursed and stalked away, dragging a hand through the short locks of her blond hair. She quickly returned to his side, however, and softly whispered, "Not a word about where we're going."

"Mitch? What was that? I couldn't hear you," Lucia said.

"Can you establish secure communications again?"

"We're trying. For now we've got to keep to these temporary numbers and e-mail accounts."

"Are you at the main headquarters in Paris?" Mitch asked and she heard Lucia's abrupt, "Yes for now."

Dani scowled. Someone within the Lazlo Group clearly had the ability to access their secure connections, but they were no closer to knowing who than before, unless…

"Dani and I will call later with our location."

Dani waved her hands as Mitch disconnected and shut off the cell phone.

"We can't tell her—"

"We can if it's not where we are. Anywhere you want to send your friends at SNAKE?"

Dani smiled. Now that was a plan. "I'm sure we can think of somewhere interesting."

The sun deliciously warmed her as they drove along in the Spider, top down, the wind ruffling the short strands of her now-blond hair. Alegria's country villa was about an hour north of Tarquinia, on Lago di Bolsena near Viterbo.

They discussed Lucia's rather sparse report, which had provided her no comfort. "If Jared Williams is the one feeding info to Jenkins and/or Breckenridge and/or someone at SNAKE, who's feeding him info?"

"Someone at Lazlo," Mitch answered and half turned in the passenger seat.

"But only Lucia and Corbett supposedly had the information, right?"

"Right," he confirmed, but then paused for a moment before he added, "But there's key support staff who would be aware of the fact that we were working on a case."

"Like who?" She squinted against the midday sun as they drove eastward toward Viterbo.

"Accounting department, possibly. They'd be advancing funds or have access to credit card charges. IT staff for another." Mitch popped open the glove compartment and unearthed a pair of dusty Ray·Bans. He wiped them off with his shirt and handed them to her.

"We need Lucia to provide all those names. We may find a connection to one of our suspects. Thanks, by the way," she said as she slipped on the sunglasses.

"I'll ask her next time we call. In the meantime, how do you plan on getting Olivia Alegria to talk to us?"

"The old-fashioned way—we're going to march right up to her door and knock."

The first rap on the door got it slammed in their faces by a rather stern-looking butler.

Their second attempt fared better as Dani flashed an old SIS badge in the dour butler's face, followed by Mitch producing an ID with the Lazlo Group's green-and-gold logo. That prompted an alarmed double-take before the butler ushered them into the foyer of the old stone farmhouse, resting on a small rise that overlooked Lago di Balseno.

As the minutes ticked by and Olivia Alegria failed to

appear after the butler's departure, Mitch shot her a dubious look. "How long before—"

"'*Scusi*," said the young woman who sashayed into the foyer, hand held out in welcome. Her toned body was wrapped in a shirt-dress of fine Italian silk, and her stiletto heels added quite a few inches to her already close to six-foot height. Long chestnut hair draped artfully across the ample curves of her body.

"Mrs. Alegria, I trust," Mitch said as he shook her hand and broadly smiled, clearly taken by the attractive woman.

"*Si*, and you would be?" she asked as she shook Dani's hand.

"Danielle Cavanaugh and Mitchell Mars. From the Lazlo Group. If you don't mind, we'd like to talk to you about your husband's death," Dani said and tamped down her annoyance at Mitch's reaction.

"*Va bene*, although when Corbett called to say there were some problems, I assumed you were delaying any further investigation," Olivia said and motioned for them to follow her.

She led them to a back sunroom, which overlooked a gorgeous pool and a hillside that sloped downward, providing a clear view of the crystal-blue lake and woods surrounding the old stone villa. The sunroom furniture consisted of ornate pieces in painted wrought iron.

The butler was already pouring them coffees as they took seats around the marble-topped table in the middle of the room.

Olivia immediately picked up her small espresso cup, tossed in the lemon rind and took a dainty sip. "So, have you reopened the investigation?"

"Possibly. We understand you had concerns about the funding of the foundation that had chosen your husband as its spokesperson," Dani began, picking up a cup of coffee and likewise taking a sip of the strong brew.

"Sergio was very excited to be honored, but then something happened. I don't know what. He was quite upset about it. A week later, he lost control of his car and was killed." Pain filled her gaze, and the espresso cup rattled against the saucer as she placed it there.

"Sergio was an excellent driver. The roads were clear that night and he always kept that Lamborghini in top shape," she added.

"The police report indicated that he might have fallen asleep at the wheel," Mitch noted, but Olivia waved off that suggestion.

"He crashed just a few miles from the house, and when he left here he was wide awake."

Dani shot Mitch a glance, as if wondering just how far to push it, but then she asked, "You and Sergio lived quite well. You have this home and others like it. Also, the Lamborghini he crashed, and if I know my cars, a rather pricey vintage Ferrari is sitting in the drive along with a Rolls."

Olivia's nonreaction spoke volumes. "Sergio made good money as a soccer player, but all this comes courtesy of my family's inheritance. But I do think Sergio's death was about money—the foundation's money. At the time of his death I hadn't made the connection."

"But you hired the Lazlo Group to investigate the foundation months after—" Mitch began, but Olivia immediately jumped in with, "*Si* because first I called Barrett Jenkins about the money."

Dani shook her head, puzzled. "Jenkins isn't on the board nor involved with the foundation in any capacity."

Olivia wagged a finger, as if chastising her. "He may not be listed, but he had his hands in the mix. Sergio told me he was responsible for John Breckenridge's education foundation getting a rather large donation."

The photo and story on the Web site had confirmed the donation, but had not hinted at any involvement on the part of Jenkins. "Are you sure?"

Olivia shrugged. "No. It was what Sergio told me. He had wanted the money to start a soccer camp for underprivileged children but Breckenridge got the money instead."

Mitch pressed the point. "So that's when he became angry—"

"No, the real anger came later," Olivia explained. "At least a week or more after that. He had met with someone at the foundation for lunch to discuss the situation. When he came home he was…*como se dice arrabiato?*"

"Enraged," Dani supplied for her. "What about?"

"He wouldn't say. I suspected at the time it was because they had refused to reconsider his request for money for the camp."

"Do you know who your husband met?" Mitch asked.

Olivia polished off the remainder of the espresso and her hands shook as she laid the cup on the table. "No, I don't. A week later, Sergio was gone."

"I'm sorry, Mrs. Alegria. I imagine it was quite a blow," Mitch said. Olivia shook her head and looked away, tears threatening in her eyes. She dragged a hand through her hair rather theatrically, but there was no doubt about the real emotion in her voice as she said, "How can you know what it's like to lose the love of your life?"

Mitch's gaze settled on Dani, causing an unexpected and unwelcome flutter in the region of her heart. He knew, as did she. Rising to avoid further issues, Dani said, "*Grazie per parlare con noi.* We would appreciate you not mentioning this visit to anyone. We will be sure to contact you with any more information we have."

"*Grazie.* Again, so sorry for your loss," Mitch said awkwardly as he rose, leaving Olivia alone to her grief.

Once they were on the steps outside, Mitch turned to her and said, "What's the game plan?"

Dani peered upward at the sunny afternoon sky. They would have some time before night fell and could put even more distance between themselves and Rome. Plus, it seemed like many of their clues pointed toward England right now which Williams, Jenkins and Breckenridge all called home. Since all were emerging as major players in whatever was happening, it was best they head there as soon as possible.

"I don't know about you, but I think it's time we visited jolly ol' England."

"Totally agree, but we also need to dig a little more into this foundation and how or why it ties into Kruger and the rest of our suspects."

With a quick look at her watch, she said, "Perugia's about an hour away. There's a small airport there where we might be able to catch a flight to London."

"Let's go," he said and held out his hand for the keys. "My turn to drive."

"Control freak," she said, but handed him the keys anyway.

Troy's computer guru had been able to track the Ducati as far as the Viterbo area using the *autostrada* computer images. Troy didn't need any other information to know where the Sparrow was headed—Olivia Alegria's country estate.

He had intended to finish the job himself, but his mother had suddenly insisted on his presence at a soiree she was hosting that night. Her sometimes escort, John Trip, had had a sudden change of plans, according to Cassandra.

He chuckled at her lack of guile when it came to him. He

was well aware of the fact that besides being her regular lover, Trip was her assassin of choice. He had no doubt that Trip was already on the job of tracking down the Sparrow, and he had every intention of helping.

He dialed Trip's number and when the man answered he said, "I think I can assist you with the job Maman just hired you for."

"Really, Troy? Mama's finally letting you get your hands dirty?" the man replied, cynicism dripping from every word.

He bit back his annoyance. One day he'd take John Trip down a peg or two. "It's going to cost you."

"Now that's funny. Mama's paying me and I'm supposed to fork it back over to you?"

He could hear the sounds of traffic in the background and wondered whether Trip was already in Rome. "They've already left the city. You're wasting your time there."

"I suppose you've got a line on—"

"They stole a Ducati from your predecessor."

"How fancy. My predecessor. You mean the poor bastard with the bullet hole in the middle of his forehead?" A loud horn blast created static on the line for a moment before Trip said, "Is that your handiwork, little man?"

Heat suffused Troy's face, but he wouldn't let Trip's goading get to him. "Do you want the info or not? Asking price is $25,000."

A long pause followed, but then Trip said, "Not a bad amount if it'll save me some time."

"They were headed to the Viterbo area. I suspect to see Olivia Alegria. You remember her husband, don't you?" Although he knew Trip would more than remember. He had been the one to arrange for the accident involving Alegria and his Lamborghini.

"Good footballer. Shame to lose such a great car," said Trip.

"They'll be in the area. You may already be too late to catch them."

"If you're right, I'll pay you the money for saving me some time," Trip said and hung up.

Troy wasn't about to leave anything to chance. Once again calling his computer guru, he gave him the address for Olivia Alegria's country estate and asked him to check all the available satellite images. The Sparrow and her mate weren't about to hang on to the Ducati. It would be too conspicuous. He was certain they had switched to something else.

Once he had more information, he would call Trip again with another offer. After all, he couldn't rely on his mother paying his way forever, could he?

Chapter 18

Dani and Mitch left the Fiat more than a mile away from the hotel in Perugia where they had checked in, hoping to throw off anyone who might have trailed them that far. There was a small airport nearby and they hoped to get a flight out the next day. As an added precaution, they purchased yet more hair dye—jet-black for Mitch and a light auburn, almost strawberry-blond, for Dani—along with a few changes of clothes and a small duffel to replace the items they had left behind in Rome.

By the time they reached the hotel, Dani had a stitch in her injured side. Unfortunately, Mitch noticed, but before he could say a word, she said, "I'm okay. Much better than yesterday."

Mitch raised his hands in surrender. "I didn't say a thing."

"Good. Don't."

Inside the hotel room, they immediately went to work

setting up their computers and then getting down to research-ing the foundation and one and all connected with it. A couple of hours passed, and in order to lay low and not lose time, they ordered room service.

When the knock came at the door, Mitch cracked it only enough to sign the bill so that the waiter wouldn't see their computers and papers. He waited for the server to leave before bringing the meal indoors.

Dani rose slowly from her chair, her side protesting the motion, but she ignored the pull and walked to where Mitch was setting up the dishes on a small circular table. "Smells great."

"Hopefully it'll taste as good. I'm famished."

They hadn't eaten since the food Mitch had pilfered from the farmhouse for breakfast. Which brought a reminder of something else they hadn't done since that morning. "When do we check in with Lucia again?"

"We'll send her another number after dinner. See what they've managed to find out."

"You don't trust that the communications won't be com-promised again?" she said, even as she was helping set the table and lay out the two different dishes they had ordered—crepes filled with mushrooms and cheese, and lamb chops with truffles. The Umbrian area was known for its woodland fungi, and Dani had convinced Mitch—who leaned more toward meat and potatoes—to share the differ-ent dishes.

As she sat at the table, Mitch poured them Sagrantino, a robust red wine that, she discovered as they ate, was the perfect choice for the stronger flavors of the mushrooms, truffles and lamb. As they had done in the past, they sat close together, sampling from each other's plates and sipping on the wine until they had finished the bottle.

When the meal was done, Dani leaned back and rubbed her full belly. "That was good."

Mitch's gaze drifted from her hand on her midsection upward, causing heat to rush across her cheeks, but then he immediately pushed back from the table and headed to the computers.

Dani was glad for his absence. The proximity during dinner and falling back too quickly into the routines of old was dangerous. It called to mind all the expectations of what she had once hoped for with Mitch.

She placed the plates back on the serving cart so that the table would be free in case they needed it. Then she approached Mitch, who had turned on the second cell phone. She had barely reached him when it rang.

"That was quick."

"Lucia leaves nothing to chance," he said, shooting her a glance over his shoulder.

"What have you got for us?" he said and a tinny voice responded, "Not a lot. Corbett and I have set up an independent server here at a secure location."

Dani sat on the edge of the table and looked at the setup Mitch had rigged so they would have a speakerphone on the cheap prepaid cell phone they had picked up that morning. Wires ran from the earpiece on the set to his laptop and its speakers.

"No connections whatsoever to any other Lazlo networks or staff?" Dani pressed.

"None. I've set this one up myself and it's totally stand alone. Corbett and I will be calling you with prepaid cell phones as well. All paid for in cash."

"Good," Mitch said. "We'll need a list of all support staff in the accounting and technology sectors from you, Lucia. We'll also need you to start running background checks on everyone."

Lucia sputtered a protest. "You can't think someone—"

"We have to consider every possibility. Some of these people have the greatest access in the group. They know who is where and when because they process the money and the data," she said, and when Lucia's tired sigh filtered across the line, she knew that Lucia realized they were right.

"I'm on it. Personally. Well, together with—"

"Me, my lad. Dani. It's good to hear from both of you," Corbett Lazlo said as he came on the line. "How are you feeling, Dani?"

"I'm fine, Corbett. Nothing wrong with me." She shot Mitch a glare to warn him to say otherwise.

"Mitch?" Corbett pressed.

"The lady says she's fine so I'm running with that."

Lazlo *hmmed*, as if well aware of the real situation.

"Fill me in on what you know," Lazlo instructed and between the two of them, they detailed the incidents of the day before and their visit to Olivia Alegria.

"I would gain more information from my sources for you—"

"But we don't know if they're part of the problem," Dani finished for him.

"No, we don't. For now, Lucia and I will check the support staff as well as try to run down any leads we have on Williams, Jenkins and Breckenridge." Corbett paused for a second before he tacked on, "And of course my old friends at SIS. I'm more sure than ever that one of them has some connection to all this."

"We'll call from…Milan," Mitch said and broke off the connection.

Dani chuckled. "Milan? What about Siberia or Uzbekistan or some other far-off place?"

"Unrealistic, wouldn't you say?" Mitch rose and stretched, then said, "Disguise time?"

She grimaced at the thought of the smelly hair dyes and what they were doing to her hair, but the thought of a nice long bath before they got back to work was all the incentive she needed. Grabbing hold of his hand, she said, "Come on. I'll do you first."

"You sweet-talker, you," Mitch teased, but followed her into the tight quarters of the bathroom. He put down the toilet seat cover and plopped onto it, leaned his head back so that it rested on the edge of the porcelain sink. "Do me," he said with a wink.

Do him! Unfortunately, the earlier dinner and his teasing had resuscitated one too many images of just that. But, as she had told herself from the first, being like Lazarus didn't mean they were the same as they used to be. That their feelings for one another were the same—although their desire for one another was still there.

As she wet his hair, running her fingers through those familiar strands, she repeated a warning to herself over and over not to lose sight of the bigger picture. Slipping on the gloves that had come with the hair dye, she worked it into the strands. Wrinkling her nose at its odor as she counted down the minutes until it would have to come out.

When it was close to the time, she tested a small piece of a strand, pleased to see that the color had taken. Once again she rinsed his hair, removing all the dye, then said, "Hold on a sec while I shampoo it."

She worked in the shampoo; the almond scent was fragrant. The thick lather felt heavy and luxurious on her fingers and in his hair. She massaged his scalp and he sighed with pleasure.

"Feels good," he murmured, his big body relaxed as she worked on him.

"Hmm," she said, losing herself in the simple task and the intimacy of the moment. When she was done, she almost regretted being finished since it had been so restful.

She handed him a towel, and he rubbed it through the strands of his hair as he rose and faced her.

The shock of the color faded quickly as she realized how the black accented the slate-gray of his eyes. The contrast of the dark hair with Mitch's light eyes made him even more appealing.

"You okay?" he asked, and she brushed past him, sat on the toilet bowl so that Mitch could color her hair.

"My turn," she replied, not wanting to give in to the attraction that rose up faster than she cared to admit.

Closing her eyes against the sight of him, she braced her head on the edge of the sink, but battled for balance to keep her position from aggravating her side. Mitch must have sensed the tension in her body.

"Side bothering you?"

"A little," she admitted, and the cool of the hair dye against her scalp made her jump.

"Relax," he urged, his breath warm against the shell of her ear, surprising her with his proximity.

Relax, as if she could between the pain in her side, the press of his hip against her shoulder as he labored and his fingers working the dye into the short strands of her hair.

By the time Mitch rinsed out the color, beads of sweat had popped out on her upper lip, and the pain in her side had grown exponentially. "I need to get up," she said, not even waiting for him to hand her a towel.

Water dripped down her neck before she snagged a towel from the rack and faced Mitch.

"Why don't we run a bath? The heat will help your side, and we could shampoo your hair."

We. That simple "we" and the imagining of her and him and the bath brought a rush of heat into her body. Reason said to tell him "No," but somehow her brain shut down and she mumbled, "Okay."

Mitch schooled his surprise at Dani's acquiescence but wasn't about to question it. He immediately went to the tub and got a bath going. For extra protection, he spilled in the entire bottle of bath gel the hotel provided. Bubbles would provide adequate cover. Cover being essential to avoid making another mistake tonight. Bad enough that some part of his brain had shut down and offered up the shampoo and bath in the first place.

Luckily, despite the age of the hotel, the water pressure was exceptional and the bath filled quickly. The gel perfumed the air with something floral and brought forth mounds of bubbles.

Bubbles were good, he thought again as he caught a glimpse of a naked Dani slipping beneath those bubbles.

Only a glimpse, but enough of a peek of gorgeous, smooth ass to make him itch to touch more than just the now light auburn shag of her hair. Fisting his hands, he kneeled beside the tub.

Dani had leaned back against the edge, eyes closed, her body safely concealed beneath the bubbles. She peered at him through one half-opened eye. "Can I soak for a bit? This feels heavenly."

Soak. Yes, a soak would help loosen her muscles. Reduce any discomfort in her side. Reduce the bubbles, his brain reminded him, but he agreed to her request and bolted from the bathroom.

Outside, he walked to the serving cart where his wineglass sat, empty. But the bottle of Sangrantina still held a little, and he poured it out. Barely a mouthful, but it would have to do to brace himself for his return to the bathroom.

He paced in the room, counting down the minutes. Telling himself that it would be better for both of them if he didn't return. He should just sit back down at the table with the laptops and work on getting more information on their suspects. Fists clenched, he went to the table, determined to sit, but then temptation won out.

Stalking to the door, he knocked and heard her muffled, "Come in."

As he entered, he realized that she had already tried to shampoo her hair, but was having problems—the pulled muscle hampered her ability to fully raise one arm above her head. She was awkwardly trying to work up a lather with one hand. Luckily, bubble coverage still provided some protection from temptation.

"Let me," he said, kneeling by the edge of the tub and replacing her hand with his. He worked up a lather, probing his fingers against her scalp until she closed her eyes and said, "Feels good."

He lingered, wanting her to relax and enjoy. Maybe subconsciously recognizing that with each minute that passed, the protection of the bubbles ebbed. By the time he was scooping his hands and using the water to rinse out the shampoo, he had a clear view of her amazing body, and his reacted accordingly.

When Dani slicked back her hair with her hand and met Mitch's gaze, she knew just what had his attention.

A throb began between her legs as his gaze settled on her breasts. Her nipples tightened in anticipation of his touch. She had to admit it then—she wanted his touch much as she had the other night. No matter how much she wanted to deny that he still held any sway over her emotions, there was no denying he still held control over her body.

But then, he wasn't unaffected. She didn't need to peer over the edge of the tub to know he was aroused. It was there in the way the color of his eyes had darkened and his mouth had dropped open a little. It was in the shaky breath he took and the tremble in his hands as he laid them on the edge of the tub.

"Dani, love. We both know—"

"This would be another big mistake. The other night. Now. It'll bring nothing but problems, right?" she said, wanting him to agree and back away.

Instead, he eased his hand into the water and cupped her breast. Ran his thumb over her distended nipple. "Right. A problem, but we're problem solvers, aren't we?"

She sucked in a breath and bit her lower lip as he took her nipple between his thumb and forefinger and tenderly rotated it. Fighting her desire, she said, "Other people's problems. Somehow we can't solve our own."

"Maybe because we're giving it too much thought. Maybe we should just see where this all takes us," he said, moving his hand away from her breast and up to cup the side of her face. He leaned closer, until his lips were barely an inch from hers.

"What if it doesn't take us anywhere?" She laid her hand on the side of his face and then upward, into the still-damp strands of his now way-short hair.

"How can we know if we don't start the journey?"

Chapter 19

The moan escaped from her mouth as she closed the distance and kissed him. His lips were pliant beneath hers, and it took the barest pressure of her tongue at the seam of his mouth for him to open and deepen the kiss.

Over and over she tasted his lips and danced her tongue with his, her hand at the nape of his neck to keep him close, but his hand moved downward, found the hard tip of her breast again. He rotated her nipple between his fingers until her breath exploded roughly against his lips. He took that as a further invitation and trailed his hand down her body.

She parted her legs, the warmth of the water welcome. The slow slide of his fingers into her, slick and hard. Sucking in a rough breath, she laid her hands on his shoulders and he nuzzled the side of her face, his beard rough. His whisper tickled her ear. "Do you know how hard I am for you?"

"How hard?" she asked, even as his fingers drew her closer and closer to the edge.

"There's only way to find out," he said, but made no move to stop his caresses between her legs.

She was throbbing, her muscles drawing down on his fingers and he groaned, dropped a kiss on the side of her face and then once again whispered, "Let me in, Dani. I want to feel you around me."

His words pulled her ever closer to release, but much as he wanted to feel her, she wanted him. Inside. Buried deep. His skin against hers. Her body was trembling and on the edge, but somehow she managed to undo the buttons on his shirt and slip her hand within. Beneath her palm, his nipple was hard and she tweaked it, drawing a rumbly moan from him.

She couldn't wait, and even though it meant interrupting the wonderful thrust of his fingers, she ripped the shirt off him and said, "Please join me, Mitch."

He didn't waste any time. With wet fumbling fingers, he unfastened his jeans and pushed them off.

Her mouth watered at the sight of him as he stood there, male magnificence at its best. Broad shoulders tapered to a lean muscled waist. She skipped over his erection because it would be too tempting at that moment and instead appreciated his thick thighs and long, nicely shaped legs. Hell, the man even had great feet, she thought, a moment before she allowed herself that look and more.

She reached up and covered the head of him, her hand warm from the water and slick against the smooth flesh. He groaned and clenched his fists, fighting for control. Control she wanted to break, she thought, as she slowly stroked him with one hand and cupped him with the other. He swelled, and she gently caressed that spot with her knuckles and felt him grow hard there as well. He reached down, stopped her hand.

He opened his eyes then and met her gaze, and she said, "Touch yourself."

"Damn, Dani—"

"Because I'm going to touch myself until you're ready to climb in here with me," she said and pulled her hands away from him. She brought one to her breast and played with her nipple while she slipped the other between her legs.

She watched him as he stroked himself, but he was watching her as she rubbed her fingers against the nub between her legs. His strokes became faster, more urgent, as did hers, until she complained, "Water's getting cool, Mitch."

Mitch moved quickly then, stepping into the bath and then to his knees between her legs. She braced her hands on either side of the old tub and spread her legs wide and Mitch didn't wait any longer to guide himself to her and slide inside.

The water might be getting cool, but Dani wasn't, Mitch thought as her warmth and wet surrounded him. He gritted his teeth against the feeling, but Dani laid a hand on his shoulder and then on his face. "Kiss me, Mitch."

He bent his head and kissed her as she asked, his mouth moving on hers gently as he filled her, unwilling to move because it just felt too damn good to be inside. Instead, he explored her mouth, slipping his tongue in and stroking it against hers. Bringing one hand down to the tip of her breast as he did so.

Her nipple was hard against his palm. Her breast full as he held it in his hand.

She licked the edge of his lip and whispered, "You want to touch, so touch me."

He groaned and laid his forehead against hers, looked

down to her breast, creamy against the darker color of his tanned hand except at the tip where her nipple was caramel colored with a rosy flush from the warmth of the water. The problem was, he didn't just want to touch. He wanted to taste as well.

He bent his head and took the hard tip into his mouth and sucked. She held his head to her and as he tugged on her nipple, he felt the answering pull of her muscles, milking him. Pulling him deep into her.

Dani wrapped her arms around his shoulders and held on tight as the feel of his mouth and his body dragged her away from the reality of their world and into one filled only with pleasure and the love in the tender caress of his mouth and then of his hands as he somehow reversed their positions in the bath and she was suddenly above him. Riding him.

Dani didn't mind. It let Mitch focus fully on her breasts and deepened the thrust of his thick heat into her. She didn't move at first, nearly overwhelmed by the feel of everything about him. About the way he made her feel physically. About the pleasure he brought her.

About the security and comfort he brought her heart as she held onto him. In the three years he had been gone, she had been without her rock. Without him, but now here he was again and she wasn't about to waste a moment of it even though at the end of the journey they had begun, they might find themselves walking down different paths to reach home.

She blanked that from her mind and instead gave herself over to his caresses. Held him and kissed his forehead, urged him on with gentle endearments and the slow shift of her hips.

He must have died, Mitch thought. Nothing could feel this good on earth. Dani's wet slick skin and the heat of her body as she moved on him, languidly at first, but then increasing in speed until her body was trembling and he was shaking as well.

Wrapping his arm around her waist, he slowed her pace, but helped her along by thrusting upward until the first wave of her climax rolled across her body and traveled to his. Surrounding him and drawing him in. Creating an answering ripple in his body.

He held her tightly and she gripped him just as intently, their hips grazing against one another, increasing that wave of pleasure, ebbing back and forth between them until it was impossible to contain it anymore and it crashed over them, leaving them both shuddering and breathless in each other's arms.

What do you do after having the most incredible sex of your adult life?

You go back to trying to find out who wanted you dead, Dani thought.

They sat side by the side at their computers, knees occasionally brushing as did their hands while they reached for papers or exchanged the information they had gleaned on their three suspects. As Dani considered all they had before them, it occurred to her that it connected the men to some degree. She could easily picture Williams providing Jenkins information and in turn, Jenkins providing that material to Breckenridge. Having the inside track to confidential SIS information could possibly explain Breckenridge's quick rise to power.

But none of that on its own connected the men to SNAKE and the attacks on the Lazlo Group. As for Sergio Alegria's murder—his wife had no idea with whom he had met. Jenkins, maybe?

"You're not happy." Mitch laid a hand on her shoulder and gave a reassuring squeeze.

She bent her head and pressed her face to his hand. "There're too many pieces still missing."

"We'll find those pieces. These three have to have some connection to what's happening."

Flipping through a few more pieces of paper, Dani couldn't see it coming together for some reason. Maybe it was that she was tired and her side was barking again. Rising, she did a slow stretch and the rib wrap Mitch had put back into place gave her the support she needed. The stretch helped alleviate the slight ache.

After she stretched, she picked up the papers and jabbed the air with them. "If someone from Lazlo is feeding one of these men information—"

"My money's on Williams."

"I agree, so we should focus on him to plug the leak," she said and paced for a moment before leaning her hand with the papers on the rung of the chair next to Mitch. "So let's assume Williams is taking his info to Jenkins and Jenkins to Breckenridge."

"Doesn't scream murder and mayhem to me…yet."

"Right. We need a lot more to make a case that they're involved with SNAKE and all their illegal activities," she said and tossed the papers onto the table. "I'm going to sleep on this. Maybe I'll be able to think more clearly in the morning."

With a few quick keystrokes, she shut down her laptop and Mitch followed suit, although sleep was the farthest thing from his mind as Dani headed for the bed.

She slipped beneath the covers. He followed close behind, snuggled his body to hers and laid one arm across her waist. When she wiggled her backside against him, he slipped his hand to her midsection to still the movement rousing him again.

"Don't start something you can't finish," he warned, and her husky chuckle made his blood race through his body.

"Okay," she teased, and didn't move again but instead surprised him by saying, "When this is all over, where will you go?"

"What makes you ask?" he said, puzzled by the drastic change in temperament.

"You talked about starting a journey. Am I just a stop along the road or—"

"It's too soon to know," he admitted, and waited for her to pull away or react in anger. She did neither. Instead she just relaxed her body against him and laid her arm over his, as if to tell him that it was okay to be uncertain.

Thankful for the reprieve, he allowed himself to relax and enjoy the feel of her body. He listened to her breathing, but it didn't lengthen or slow with sleep, just kept to a regular waking pace as his did.

They were both likely too wound up about all that was happening between them and about the case.

A case that seemed to grow more convoluted and complicated, not to mention perilous. They weren't close to removing themselves from danger. That made him tighten his hold on her waist, but she didn't protest. Instead, clearly conscious of her side, she slowly turned until she faced him.

She ruffled the short strands of his newly black hair before placing her hand on his shoulder. "I guess you can't rest either."

"Too much to think about. Much like you, I guess."

"Hmm," she said and rubbed her hand across his shoulder before asking, "Is Aidan a good guy?"

"The best," Mitch answered quickly, earning a chuckle from her.

"Glad to hear it. I didn't want to have to hurt him, since Lizzy Bee seemed so taken with him."

"Is Lizzy like you, besides physically, that is?" he asked

and mimicked her actions, dragging his fingers into the short strands of her hair.

Dani shook her head. "Lizzy Bee was always the Earth Mother–type. Nothing like me."

Intrigued, Mitch examined her features as he said, "You don't see yourself being the maternal type ever?"

She shrugged and averted her gaze. "When I saw Lizzy with Aidan…I have to confess to being jealous. Wondering what it might have been like for me. Then I got shot."

He put his thumb and forefinger on her chin and applied gentle pressure until she faced him. "Being shot reminded you that you weren't like Lizzy."

She shook her head. "I'm not sure I could ever be like Lizzy."

"But you wonder?" he pressed.

"Yes, I wonder." With a fast flip and groan as it aggravated her ribs, she presented him her back and moved away, putting some distance between them.

Distance being good, he decided. Just as Dani wasn't like her sister, he suspected that he wasn't like his friend Aidan, who had given up the excitement and adventure of working for Corbett Lazlo for hearth and home in Dani's small hometown.

Nope, he liked the business too much, death notwithstanding, he told himself.

He suspected Dani felt much the same, which made him consider that whatever journey they had started might ultimately take them along different paths once this mission was over.

For now. He had to focus his thoughts on tomorrow's trip to England and whatever awaited them there.

Chapter 20

Satellites were a spy's best friend, Troy thought, looking over the photo showing the blond man and woman walking toward the late-model Fiat in Olivia Alegria's courtyard. He forwarded the photo to Trip's cell phone along with the bank account number for his payment.

Trip, somewhat predictable for an assassin, called him less than a minute later.

"You think this is worth money, little man?"

"Have you found any info on your own? Or maybe good ol' Maman sent you something to go on?" he riposted.

"Cassandra hasn't given me anything. She says Lazlo has locked down in a major way."

"So I guess this is worth money, then. The older Fiat should be something we can track. *J'ai mes personnes*—"

"Your people? You mean Mommy's people don't you?" Trip taunted, but Troy wasn't about to let the other man rattle him. That would be a sign of weakness, and if he was to one day take over, people needed to understand he wasn't weak.

"I'll send you more once I've gotten confirmation of payment. That is, if you want to finish your job and collect from Cassandra."

A raucous laugh erupted across the line. "You know what, Troy? You may be more like your mother than I thought."

"*Vraiment?* And why is that, Trip?" he asked, actually quite pleased with the comparison.

"Because you'd both screw anyone for money."

The cell phone went dead in his hand and rage simmered through his body. His hands shook as he shoved the slim cell phone back into his pants pocket.

His mother might have a thing for the brutish assassin, but Troy intended to exact punishment for the slur.

But first, he had to find out exactly what Trip had been referring to about Lazlo's locking down and what his mother's contact was doing about it.

Troy knocked on the door to his mother's office.

"*Entré*," she called out and he walked in, a smile on his face.

"*Bonsoir, Maman.* How are things going?" he asked, forcing innocent calm onto his features.

His mother narrowed her eyes, clearly not fooled by his demeanor.

"Tell me what you're doing, *mon fils,* and don't bother to deny it. Trip has filled me in on all that you know," she said with a flourish of her hand in the direction of the chair before her desk.

"Come now, Mother—"

"You think the Sparrow and her mate have spoken to Alegria's widow?"

He shrugged cavalierly which set his mother off. Anger drove her from her chair and to his side. She snagged a lock of blond hair and tugged. "Tell me, Troy."

"Will you tell me what your Lazlo contact said?" He winced as she yanked his hair again but didn't budge, and so she relented, almost seeming to admire his spunk.

"Corbett knows there's a leak. He's playing this one very close to the vest."

"Your contact—"

"I know you'd like me to tell you who it is. Maybe you even think you can pay them more for their information. Use that against me." She slapped him hard across the face.

Troy felt the dull flush creep up his face but didn't react to the blow. Instead, he faced her, challenge in his gaze. "Why can't you trust me? If I'm to one day run—"

"Who says I will pick you to be my successor?" she immediately countered, obviously wanting to cut him down. His mother must fear that if he got too full of himself, she would never be able to control him.

"Like your father chose your brother? But he died, clearing the way for you. Or was your father going to choose someone else even after that?"

His mother's face went cold, and he knew why. His words hit home too accurately. Her father had never forgiven her for his son's death at the hands of Corbett Lazlo.

Troy had heard the rumors that because of that, her father had been ready to turn over the family business to someone else. But Cassandra had taken care of that, much as he suspected she would take care of Corbett, and even him if she had to.

No one would keep his mother from being in control of the multi-faceted organization that had been her life since the death of her beloved brother. Since wresting control from her father on his death bed.

No one. Except maybe him.

Morning found Dani sandwiched to Mitch, his erection pressing into her belly. She shifted against him, half-asleep, and he murmured something groggily but reached up and unerringly found the tip of her breast beneath the thin cotton of the T-shirt she had worn to bed.

His hand was sleep-warm.

She returned the favor, finding him beneath the loose fleece of the sweats he had donned. Her movements were slow but determined as she stroked him until, between her own legs, she felt the wetness of her rising need and the ache of emptiness.

Easing the fleece downward, she freed him, eased her thigh over his and guided him to her center.

He finally opened his eyes, glanced downward and watched as he flexed his hips and slipped home. He brought one big hand around to the small of her back and pressed her close, increasing his penetration, but he didn't move.

She didn't want him to, she thought, easing her hand beneath his T-shirt to reach up and finger his nipple, dragging a protest from him.

"You know what that does to me," he groaned, bent his head and kissed her.

"I do," she whispered, and for good measure, tweaked the hard pap between her fingers. Inside her, he jumped and swelled in pleasure.

"Not fair," he said and moved his hand upward and copied her actions, pulling and tweaking at her nipple.

As he thickened inside her, she clenched her muscles on

him, felt her own answering throb and pull until with a sudden explosion, her climax rushed over her.

His body jerked against hers, and he muttered a muffled curse as he lost control and spilled himself within her.

Afterward, they rose, silent, as if trying to deny that the pleasure between them was about something more than physical release. About physical need for one another.

With the airport nearby and the Fiat ditched at a distance, they hailed a cab.

Dani was eager to be on her way to England and away from Italy. The country held too many disturbing memories for both of them. Maybe once they were in London they could regain perspective and deal with what had happened in the course of the past few days.

Maybe in London she could control herself and stop jumping Mitch's bones.

As she sat beside him in the cab and shot a look at him, she noted the tense line of his jaw. The way his hands were clenched into fists and rested on his thighs.

She remembered his regretful curse as he had come that morning.

She worried she was falling in love with him again and that was so not a good thing.

As she had told him the night before, she didn't think she was like her sister, Lizzy. She couldn't be—not until she had settled all the unfinished business in her life.

Finding her parents' killers and bringing them to justice.

Finding those responsible for what had happened to her and Mitch.

The voice in her head reminded her of where vengeance had gotten her the last time—nearly dead. Dead to her sister until this threat was over.

Only then could she truly rise like Lazarus and resume her normal life.

Not that her life had been normal, she thought, and, unbidden, she felt a yearning for normal. For the kind of life she imagined her sister had—happy, calm and filled with love.

Risking another glance at Mitch, she asked herself if he could ever give up his life for normal.

Sadly, she suspected the answer was no.

Troy smiled as he reviewed the satellite image he had sent late the night before to Trip—one of the Fiat sitting not far from the Piazza Matteotti. Of course, that didn't mean the occupants where anywhere nearby, Troy thought.

His cell phone rang. Trip was calling.

"You found them," he said with satisfaction.

"Sorry, little man. The hood's ice-cold and damp with the early morning dew. The car's been sitting here all night."

Perugia was out of the way, and except for its chocolates, not the kind of place one would go unless...

They could connect to the trains and buses there, but that would make for a slow getaway from Italy. He had no doubt that's what the Sparrow wanted to do—put distance between herself and the kills in Rome. Too bad she didn't realize that she couldn't outrun him.

"Do you think they're laying low for a few days? Maybe she was injured during the Rome shooting," he said.

Trip barked a laugh. "Your mommy's contact says my predecessor winged the Sparrow."

Troy thought about the satellite photo he had sent earlier. The woman in the picture hadn't seemed injured.

"I don't think Cassandra's contact is correct so there's no

need to check the hospitals or other places someone might go for medical attention."

Which brought him back to his original thinking—the Sparrow was getting ready to fly this nest.

Fly…

He recalled that Perugia had been developing its airport since many years back. There were even commercial flights to various countries thanks to a carrier that had opened business earlier that year.

"There's a small airfield nearby. They're probably trying to get out of Italy as quickly as possible."

Trip grunted. "For your sake, let's hope you're right. Otherwise, I'll take my wasted time out of your hide next time I visit your mommy."

Chapter 21

The cab deposited them at the sole terminal at the airport.

Mitch took the lead, guiding Dani away from the main entrance and to the farthest edge of the building. She noticed a large black Jeep sitting at the opposite end of the terminal. Something about it raised her suspicions.

She pulled Mitch around the corner of the building and at his puzzled look, said, "Jeep at the far end."

He nodded and peered back around the corner.

Observing the cars passing by their end of the terminal—the direction one would have to go to exit the airport or access parking—she didn't see the Jeep drive by. Poking her head around the corner, she realized the vehicle was gone.

Or maybe it was your imagination seeing demons? she said to herself.

They hadn't said a word to Corbett and Lucia about where they really were and had kept their calls on the prepaid cell phones to a minimum, which would have made it nearly impossible for them to be tracked. Despite that, she knew their passage from Rome could have been monitored. The proliferation of cameras everywhere along the roadways and city streets made it possible for someone to have tracked them on the Ducati. The bike had been the handiest and speediest vehicle for a quick exit, but fairly noticeable.

But from there...

Had someone seen them at the Alegria estate? Or was it possible the butler had spoken to someone. That would be rich. The old *the-butler-did-it* joke.

"Dani?" Mitch asked from beside her and inclined his head in the direction of the various hangars along the edge of one runway.

She glanced at her watch. The timetables on the Internet said there wasn't a commercial flight for some time. Too much time to waste and be exposed while sitting in the terminal. The hangars housed a host of private planes and charter air companies. One of them might provide the ticket they needed to London.

"Let's personally check out a charter."

Security was at a minimum at the airport. They easily slipped past a large gap in the chain-link fence and raced across an open stretch of tarmac to the first hangar.

The doors of the hangar were open, revealing two small planes within, but no one was in attendance. Mitch walked up to the first plane and smiled.

"Cessna Turbo Skylane. Good power and it's got the range to get us there."

Dani walked up to him as he ran his hand over the red and gray lines on the shell of the plane and toward the door to the cockpit. "Let me guess. You can fly this thing."

"Air Force wings may be made of lead, but that doesn't mean that this poor Army boy doesn't appreciate the wonders of flight." He grinned and with a jerk of the handle, popped open the door on the cockpit, dropped the stairs into the plane and climbed in.

"All fueled up as well," he called out from behind the yoke in the cockpit.

The flash of something black and fast snared her attention. The Jeep she had seen earlier, barreling its way across the tarmac in their direction.

"Good thing. Get it going," she yelled, then bent and removed the chocks from the wheels on the plane.

She had one foot on the stairs as Mitch fiddled with some wires beneath the instrument panel. With a smile he said, "No ignition key, but these things are easier to hot-wire than a car."

As she tossed their bags behind the cockpit chairs, the engines roared to life. She climbed in, pulling up the stairs behind her and took a spot beside Mitch in the pilot's seat.

As soon as she sat, Mitch pushed the airplane forward, expertly working the controls, but even as he did so, she could see the Jeep gaining ground on them.

Mitch did as well. He steered the plane from the hangar and onto the approach for the runway.

Someone official finally noticed and came running from the adjacent hangar, waving his arms and screaming at Mitch to stop, but they couldn't. The Jeep was now just yards away and would catch up to them soon.

Mitch pressed the plane, the engines purring smoothly as he swung it onto the open runway. With the long stretch of smooth ground before them, he increased the acceleration of the plane and from behind them came the *pop-pop-pop* of gunfire and sirens.

Dani peered out one window and barely got a glimpse of the Jeep as it chased their tail followed by one police car. The two other police cars heading their way from the opposite direction were infinitely more troubling. They were angling to cut them off headfirst on the runway.

Mitch must have seen them as well. He cursed and said, "Let's see just how much climb this baby has."

He pushed to max thrust and worked the controls, getting the nose off the ground even as the Jeep pulled level with them on Dani's side of the plane. The tinted window lowered, providing her a glimpse of a man's face before the nose of an AK-47 came out and he opened fire.

The shots pinged against the metal of the plane but luckily didn't break through, and as if realizing it, the driver turned his attention to the engine, trying to inflict damage.

Sparks flew as the bullets struck the casing on the single engine but stopped as the Jeep jerked to a halt in response to the police cars now about to cross into the runway before them.

"Watch out, Mitch," she said and braced for impact, but with another long steady pull on the yoke, the nose came up even more and the plane surged over the police cars on the runway, clipping the lights on one of them with the landing gear.

"Safe for now," he said as they quickly picked up speed and climbed, although she suspected he would stay below the radar level.

"For now?" she questioned and as she looked back at the runway, she noted that the Jeep was racing away from the scene, two police cars in hot pursuit.

"Don't know how badly the gear was damaged so we may be in for a rocky landing. Plus we need to get out of Italian air space before they scramble anyone to come after us, if they even do."

"Can we do that?" Dani asked, peering down at the ground below as it rushed past her.

Mitch flipped a few switches on the instrument panel. Two high-resolution monitors displayed all the critical flight information and a precise GPS position laid over a map of their location. He shot a look at the monitors before he said, "I'm shutting off the transponder and we'll stay below radar level. That will make it harder to find us, and with this baby's air speed, we should be able to make it out of Italian airspace quickly."

"I guess we'll keep below radar level to land in England?" Someone had found out where they were, but hopefully not where they were going.

Mitch nodded and his hands tightened on the yoke. "The airports will likely be on alert to watch for us, plus we can't land this injured bird in an airport anyway."

Great, she thought. Not to mention she hated flying—an awkward thing for a jet-setting spy—and now the landing gear might shatter like dry pasta when Mitch put the plane down.

Mitch, she thought, admiring the confident way he handled the controls. He looked her way and said, "Are you okay?"

"Never better," she replied and realized it was true.

With Mitch beside her, she knew they would handle whatever came next.

Mitch watched Dani as she reviewed the assorted files and information they had gathered on all their suspects. She grew frustrated, much as she had the night before.

"You're overthinking it," he had said. She agreed and put

the laptop away, giving her concentration over to the passing countryside below.

Mitch continued monitoring the assorted dials for the plane. Luckily, whoever had shot at them had failed to do any damage. Oil, hydraulics and gas were at acceptable levels and the plane had responded well to all his commands, confirming that none of the bullets had damaged the rudder or any of the other essential components.

Now the only concern—besides the leaks at Lazlo and the assassin trying to kill them—was the landing gear.

The plane had hit hard, but only the lights on the police car. He had felt a strong shudder in the yoke as they had connected, but not much else. At least nothing of significance.

Which had left him free to concentrate on the flight and on Dani.

Dani. Dani. Dani. Maybe concern number one, because she had touched him. Both last night and again this morning as they had made love, he had wondered what it would be like if they remained partners. If they had each other's backs during other missions.

But with that thought came the knowledge that each and every mission risked their lives.

He could deal with risking his. He'd done it time and time again for his country and for Lazlo. Of course, nearly dying three years earlier had given him fresh perspective on just why he didn't want to come close to dying again.

Dani had almost died a year earlier.

Could he risk it again? Or would it make sense to try and find happiness in a small stone home along the Silvershire shore as his friend Aidan had?

He reached over and ran the back of his hand across her cheek, needing contact with a warm and very alive Dani.

She trained her gaze on him. That marvelous green-eyed gaze he had dreamed of virtually every night for the past three years. Only now it was here and real.

"Something wrong?" She sat up straighter and shot him a hesitant smile.

Her words from the night before came back to him, and inside, warmth came at the thought of having a home with her. Of waking beside her and going to sleep with her in his arms. Did she wonder about the same thing? He needed to know before he opened his heart, to her, anymore.

"When you think about whether you could live like your sister, who's beside you?"

Dani shook her head and looked away from him, clearly in avoidance mode.

With one eye on the open air ahead, he grasped her chin and tenderly urged her to face him again. "Who's there, Dani? Beside you in bed? Across from you at the table for dinner?"

Mitch needed to know, almost as much as he needed to discover who the Lazlo leak was. He wouldn't let her avoid an answer.

"Don't do this, Mitch." She jerked her head away from his touch and looked down once again at her hands, which were nervously playing with the strap on the belts holding her in the co-pilot's chair.

"Why, Dani? Why is it so hard for you to answer? You must have pictured it—"

"Because it's not you, Mitch," she nearly shouted, shocking him into silence. Rocking him with the admission.

Her hands fumbled on the closure for the belt, but then she managed to undo them and left the cockpit for the small baggage area behind.

Mitch tightened his hands on the yoke and flew on.

He had pressed for his answer and gotten it. Too bad it wasn't the answer he had wanted to hear.

Dani slinked down into the seat closest to the tail of the plane, pulled her knees up and buried her head there.

In those moments where she dared to let herself wonder, there had been only one person beside her in bed. Across the table from her at dinnertime and breakfast and even lunch.

Mitch, of course, not that she could admit it, she thought. Things were already too complicated and allowing their emotions to get out of control would make their assignment even harder. Tears came to her eyes. She let them spill over because there were too many of them to dam in. Besides, if she did that she'd get too noisy and he would know she was crying.

Crying for him, something she had thought she was done doing once she realized he was no longer dead.

So she let the tears flow unabated until she was dry. Only then did she pick up her head and wipe away the telltale tracks. By the time she returned to the cockpit, all evidence of them needed to be gone.

Emotions had no place in this mission. If anything, emotions would only compromise it. She could see Mitch hesitating from doing something he should in order to protect her and that couldn't happen.

Completing this assignment was of first and foremost importance, not daydreaming about things that might not ever be possible. Home and hearth and Mitch… No matter how her heart yearned for that, her logical side dictated that she concentrate on what was important for the now.

With her emotions in check and her list of priorities firmly acknowledged, she returned to the cockpit.

"Where do you plan to land?" she asked as she strapped herself back into the co-pilot's seat.

Mitch observed her closely, clearly trying to gauge her mood before replying, "Normally I'd try Stansted. It's a small airfield about forty-five minutes outside of London, but they'll probably be on alert for this airplane."

"What other options do we have?" she asked, back in mission-only mode and ready to consider all the variables.

"Plenty of open spaces in the countryside. A long roadway or empty field." His tone was professional, but it was impossible not to detect the worry in his voice, Dani thought. "You're afraid the landing gear might not hold up."

"We only clipped with the front landing gear, but… If it gives, we'll be off balance."

With a shake of her head, she said, "I guess we should prepare for a bumpy landing."

Chapter 22

The emerald-green fields of the West Essex hillside spread out below them. At a distance was Stansted airport, but Mitch instead looked for an area long enough and smooth enough to allow for what he hoped would be a safe landing. He had spotted one earlier and doubled back and flew over it once again before deciding it would do.

He banked the plane, making a wide turn before beginning the approach. "Make sure you're buckled in tight," he said, and for good measure, reached out and yanked on the straps of her belt.

She slapped his hand away. "I'm fine. Let's just get this bird down so we can head into town."

Dipping the nose, he worked the controls but noticed from the corner of his eye that Dani did tighten the straps and brace one arm on the wall beside her.

The plane moved ever closer to the ground, the countryside a blur around them before the first jolt as the back wheels touched down. The plane jerked up and down violently, roughly bouncing along the uneven ground. The yoke shook in his hands, but he controlled it, and together with the foot controls, brought the nose down and started to slow the plane.

Their speed had decreased substantially when the plane violently lurched to the right side. Metal groaned and crunched. The plane bucked and reeled spasmodically.

He fought to keep it from flipping and succeeded, but one bone-jarring bounce came right after another, yanking a pained grunt from Dani every time until the plane finally shuddered to a halt barely yards from the first trees in a small copse near the field's edge.

"Rough, but we're still in one piece. Thanks," Dani said, her breathing uneven and pained, one hand pressed tightly to her injured ribs.

"Sorry to add to your misery, but we've got a hike of about a mile to the closest town." He unbuckled, walked around her seat and opened the door of the cockpit. With the plane at a crazy tilt, the door nearly touched the ground. He didn't bother putting down the steps. They wouldn't do much good, and they could easily drop to the ground thanks to the plane's position.

He grabbed their bags and placed them within easy reach, jumped down onto the ground and then removed all the bags. When he reached for the last one, Dani crouched by the door, her arm wrapped around her side.

"Let me," he said, and she didn't protest his assistance as he carried her down as easily as he would a child.

Once on the ground, Mitch grabbed a small fire ax from the back of the plane and chopped some branches from the nearby trees. Together with some fallen branches and under-brush that Dani rounded up, they managed to create enough camouflage to hide the plane. Hopefully it would be a few days before anyone noticed it from the air or any of the nearby farmhouses.

They divided the bags, Dani insisting she could hold her own, but with Mitch shouldering the bigger part of the burden. He pointed toward the stand of trees. "Through here and then about a mile farther there's a small village I noticed while we were up in the air. Can you make it?"

"I can make it," she said and trudged ahead of him, her pace steady and grueling. He understood. The sooner they got away from the plane the better. Whoever had known they were in Perugia would connect the dots and know where they were headed. They were likely already looking for them in England.

Luckily it wasn't that warm a day and the walk went quickly. In less than a half hour, they were at the edge of the village. Public transportation was spotty and the local cab— the only one in town—was on a run already. Luckily a tour bus had just dropped off a group of tourists headed for a walk through the West Essex countryside. The bus man was on his way back to London and gladly offered them a ride in exchange for the few euros they had left.

Once they were settled on seats toward the back of bus to give them some privacy, he said, "Aidan and I kept a small flat as a safe house. No one knew about it except the two of us."

"Good. Maybe we can use that as our base of operations. When do you want to call Lucia?" Dani asked, and glanced out the window at the countryside, which reminded her of her Silvershire home.

"Let's wait until we're settled. She'll hopefully have a secure computer connection where we can try and find out more on Jared Williams."

"So you've decided he's to be our first target?"

"Don't get your nose of out joint," he admonished, and teasingly swiped at her nose.

"Partners, remember? We make decisions together," she reminded him, but there was little sting in her tone.

With a nod, Mitch agreed, and they were silent for the rest of the ride. When the tour bus operator dropped them off in front of Buckingham Palace, Mitch glanced at Dani and asked, "You okay with a cab to Kensington Gardens?"

She nodded and with a quick wave of her hand, flagged one down.

Luckily, traffic was light until they hit Oxford Street and the throngs of shoppers, automobiles and buses slowed them down. They remained with the cab until they got past Self-ridges, at which point Mitch told the cabbie that they were getting out.

Once on the street, Mitch explained that the flat was closer to Kensington Gardens, which meant they still had a bit of a walk coming up.

"That's okay. Better not to let anyone drop us off too close anyway," she said. They walked side-by-side as the shopping area ended and the streets became more residential. Kensington Gardens was on their left. They were a few blocks into the park when Mitch turned onto one of the side streets. Off the main drag, the area grew quieter. The homes were quaint and picturesque.

Mitch walked to the gate for one home, opened it and strolled to the door. Dani followed and chuckled as he tipped back the wrought-iron planter by the door, bent and removed a key from beneath. She hoped that meant that Aidan still owned the house.

"Very high tech," she kidded as he slipped the brass key

into the front door. Luckily it opened. Once inside, he walked up the stairs to the second story. At the door there, he once again inserted the key, but once the door was open, the *beep-beep-beep* from within warned of an alarm.

He punched in at least eight numbers and the alarm quieted. Once she walked in, he reset the security system behind them.

It was musty within, probably a testament to how long anyone had been there, Dani thought and viewed the small flat. A combo dining/living room area and beyond that, bedroom, bathroom and galley-style kitchen. Serviceable as a bachelor flat, she thought.

Mitch had walked to the back of the room and kicked on a small window air conditioner. He disappeared into the bedroom for a second, and she heard the second thrum of another unit coming to life.

When he walked back out, he grabbed their bags and brought them to the dining room table. "The cable modem router is nearby. We'll get the best signal here."

She helped him unpack everything and assemble the make-shift speaker phone once again. Seated by his side, they called Lucia and Corbett. They answered immediately.

"Milan, huh? So you two had nothing to do with that stolen Cessna in Perugia this morning or the wild police chase?" Lucia immediately said.

"Did the police—"

"Driver of the Jeep got away after the police cars crashed into each other."

"What else have you got for us?" he asked.

"Another secure link into SIS. I'm e-mailing it to your private account. We've already tapped into it to get some more info on Williams. I'll e-mail that as well so you can keep your hacking to a minimum."

"Thanks, Lucia. What about your review of Lazlo staff?" she asked, concerned that despite their best efforts someone within the organization would reveal something vital to their enemies.

"We've isolated about half a dozen candidates who had high enough clearance. I'm sending a link to all that information in a second e-mail."

Dani looked at Mitch. His brow was furrowed and he rubbed one finger across his lips, deep in thought. When he turned his gaze on hers, she knew what he was thinking. "We want to set a trap, Lucia. Can you help us?"

"Just tell me what you need."

Troy had heard the car pull up in the driveway of their palatial mansion. Drawing aside the drapes at his window, he watched as Trip eased from the car and walked up to the door. It opened quickly and the assassin entered.

Interesting, he thought and powered up his laptop, wondering at the reason for the assassin's late-night visit. Wondering if he had accomplished his task so quickly.

Given the hour of the night, he had no doubt that his mother wasn't taking Trip to her offices. They were regular lovers and Cassandra would probably conduct this business in her bedroom.

Perfect for him, he thought as he tuned in to the channel monitoring her room.

Trip and she were standing close and Trip handed her a box of Baci chocolates, which his mother stared at with apparent disgust.

"Is this supposed to make up for missing the mark?" she asked.

Trip grinned and laid a hand on her waist, drew her near. "No, but maybe this will. I picked it up in Milan since I had more free time than I expected," he said, and with his free hand, reached into his pocket and pulled out a diamond bracelet, which he dangled before her face.

She snagged it from his hand and held it up between her thumb and forefinger for a closer inspection. "You think jewels will do it?"

He rubbed himself against her, and her eyes closed as desire apparently drove away her anger. She tossed the bracelet to the floor and moved her hand downward as Trip said, "I hope those jewels you're heading for will do it."

"I'm not paying you until you kill her," she said, as she unzipped him and released his erection for her touch.

"I'll finish the job, but the trail is cold."

"*Vous n'êtes pas,*" she said, and Troy nearly gagged at the sex play between his mother and her favorite assassin.

But then Trip groaned and his knees started to buckle. Cassandra was obviously exacting some punishment with the hand that had slipped into his pants.

"Damn, Cass. Let go," he rasped, a grimace on his face as he sank to his knees.

She bent her head until her face was right in his. "I want her dead. I want Corbet dead. *Comprenez?*" she directed from behind clenched teeth before releasing him.

Turning on one heel, she walked toward the bed, dropping her robe as she went and adding an extra sway to her hips.

When she sat on the edge of the bed, Trip was still leaning on his hands and panting, but his eyes never left Cassandra.

She spread her legs, giving him a glimpse of her auburn curls, and anger surged through Troy at the sight.

He couldn't watch anymore and snapped off the monitor, revolted with the way his mother spread her legs for a man who had entirely screwed up his assignment. After losing them in Perugia, Cassandra had directed Trip to Milan, where he had been unable to locate them despite being given the address of the Lazlo offices and safe house.

He didn't know how his mother had gotten that information, and it galled him. But then again, her contact had provided totally useless data.

Troy had no doubt that the Sparrow and her friend had headed to London and not Milan as Cassandra's Lazlo contact had indicated. Olivia Alegria had been sure to voice her doubts about the foundation again, and this time she had clearly found a receptive ear.

Jenkins and Breckenridge were in London along with the Dumont SIS contact and possibly a connection to his family's organization. Since his mother was too busy bedding the help, he would have to take care of business himself. He told himself again that maybe if he did so, his mother would finally come to respect him.

After packing a bag, he called ahead to the small airfield they maintained outside of Paris. The man who answered sounded groggy, as if he had been asleep, but he immediately perked up when he heard Troy's voice.

"Call the pilot and have the plane ready within the hour. I'm headed to London."

Chapter 23

Midnight, and they had covered more bases than she had thought possible.

They had narrowed their list of suspects within the Lazlo group to three key people—the comptroller, Corbett Lazlo's administrative assistant and the second-in-command in the IT department. All three had access to key information and the goings on at the highest levels of the group. With Lucia and Corbett's assistance, each of them would be told a seemingly important piece of information. False information, but clearly the kind of information that was too tempting to not pass on.

The background Lucia had worked up on Jared Williams and the link into SIS had provided a wealth of details. Enough for them to stake out Williams to see if anyone passed him the false data. Hopefully he would in turn relay that information up the line, helping them pinpoint who was actually calling the shots. Maybe even who had the vendetta against the Lazlo Group.

"Someone at SIS has a gripe with Corbett. What do you think it could be about?" she asked and tilted back on the two legs of the high-backed dining room chair.

"Corbett rose up the ranks fast when he was there. Even after he was tossed, he still managed to land on his feet."

"Professional jealousy. Enough to make someone set up Kruger and all those Lazlo operatives for execution?"

Mitch nodded emphatically. "What else could it be, except maybe money?"

"So what you're saying is that money and power are the only things that matter to men like Williams and the SIS mole."

Mitch leaned back in his chair and laced his fingers behind his head, elbows outstretched, which widened the already broad expanse of his chest. With a chuckle, he said, "Most men. It's a pissing game with us, Dani. You should know that by now."

"With women being number three on the list. So maybe this mole and Lazlo had the same lady friend."

At that comment, Mitch broke into outright laughter. "Corbett and a woman? He's a man's man. A different woman on his arm for every occasion."

"So you've never known him to be involved with anyone?" she asked, rose from her chair and walked to one of the windows looking out over the avenue and in the distance, Kensington Gardens.

"No one, although…I think Lucia has a crush on him."

"Interesting. So if we're back to money and power—"

"We are, and since Corbett hasn't mentioned knowing either Jenkins or Breckenridge, then maybe we should assume that Williams is probably reporting to the SIS traitor," Mitch said and stood, coming to stand beside her.

"It's not too late for a walk in the park." He pointed toward the tops of the trees visible beyond the row of homes. A full moon illuminated them, turning the leaves a silvery green as a breeze stirred them.

She wrapped her arms around herself and shook her head. "I'm ready for sleep."

"The bedroom's—"

"I know where the bedroom is, but the couch looks pretty comfy."

"Got it," he said with a salute. "See you in the morning."

He stalked to the bedroom and closed the door behind him, but a moment later, the door opened and he tossed out the bag with their clothes.

The door slammed closed again.

Dani walked over and picked up the bag. His clothes were still in there, but she suspected he already had his own things in the apartment.

Shutting off all the lights except one small one by the couch, she stripped and slipped into one of the sweatshirts Mitch had bought in Perugia. Big and comfy, it hung to mid-thigh and smelled of him.

Self-flagellation, she told herself as she settled on the couch. A throw rested along the top of the couch and she yanked it down, covering herself with it.

As she closed her eyes, she visualized how the morning would go, imagining how they would stake out Williams's apartment in nearby Chelsea. Contemplating how they could monitor Williams once he went across town to Vauxhall Cross and the prominent SIS buildings along the River Thames.

She wondered just what they could access using the link Lucia had provided—maybe the SIS security system with all its assorted video feeds?

Note to self—talk to Lucia in the morning about the video feeds.

With that final thought, she allowed herself to drift to sleep.

Mitch pounded the pillow, unable to get comfortable.

The large king-sized bed, which had always been blissfully roomy, now seemed overly empty and way too hard.

Damn, Dani anyway. It was all her fault.

Women just complicated things for men. Way easier to just stick to the two most important things on the list— money and power.

He had plenty of money. He had managed to save most of his pay during his entire stint in the Army. Lazlo remunerated his agents well. Very, very well, and being basically frugal by nature, he had set most of that aside also.

As for power, well, he'd had enough of ordering people around in the Army. As a top agent for Lazlo, he'd had his share of control on all of his missions save one—this one.

Dani had made it clear this was a partnership with neither of them in control.

Even in bed he didn't control her, not that he minded. He liked it when Dani took charge. He regretted the thought immediately as he hardened and the bed became even lonelier and more uncomfortable.

Damn, he thought, and sat up on the edge of the bed, hanging his head in his hands as he thought of the woman on the other side of the door. Barely twenty feet away.

Actually, too far away by at least nineteen feet and eleven inches.

Surging off the edge of the bed, he stalked to the door and yanked it open. He had barely taken a step through the door when Dani popped up over the edge of the couch, her Sigma trained on him.

He picked up his hands in surrender and stopped short.

"Holy mother, Mitch. I could have shot you." She lowered the gun and dragged a hand through the short strands of her strawberry-blond hair.

If she had it probably would have saved him a lot of pain and frustration. "Sorry. I just thought it was a waste of a perfectly comfortable bed for you to be out here."

An amused grin crept to her face. "So you risked getting shot because the bed was too…big."

The emphasis on the last word made it clear she understood perfectly. *Big* being code for *lonely*. Being an admission that he needed her, if only for sex and sleeping. "Don't read anything into it, Dani."

"Right. So this is all about comfort, which means no touchie, no feelie, no nookie."

He remembered her words in the cockpit and any desire fled with the recollection. "I'm glad you can make that promise," he said to deflate her ego and regain control.

He turned and her amused chuckle chased him into the bedroom, but a second later, she came in, brushed past him and made herself comfortable in his bed.

Suppressing a grin, he walked to the far side of the bed and slipped under the covers. Pillowing his head under his hands, he said, "Good night, Dani."

"Good night, Mitch."

Before dawn they were in a van with tinted windows, sitting outside Williams's Chelsea flat. The fully equipped surveillance van, which had been painted with the logo of a local television station, had come from the garage in Mitch and Aidan's safe house. The two men clearly believed in not only having a backup plan, but in being fully prepared to execute that plan.

The garage had also had a hidden trap door which led to a room filled with an assortment of weapons. Mitch had picked a TEC-9 and a Heckler & Koch XM-8 from the small arsenal, along with ammunition for the assault rifles.

Armed and ready, they set up camp and waited. The monitors connected to the infrared thermal imaging system had pinpointed one human source of heat in the bedroom.

No activity was visible inside for a good hour, but then the parabolic-dish listening device picked up a loud electronic chirp. It sounded like a phone and not an alarm.

The infrared thermal imaging system showed Williams rising. A moment later, he said, "Hello, luv."

"Pillow talk?" she whispered, and Mitch adjusted the balance on the microphone, trying to pick up the conversation on the other end of the connection, but it wasn't possible.

"Is that so? You're sure about this, right?" Williams asked.

Garbled static came through the mike, but it was unintelligible. Williams finished up with "I miss you, too. How about you take tomorrow off? Fly up tonight and spend a long weekend with me?"

"So it's a female, but we don't know if it's our leak," he said.

"What about his being a nancy boy? Maybe he's talking to a man," she said.

"So we're no closer to eliminating one of our possible suspects." He leaned back in his chair and watched Williams move around the apartment in the monitor.

When he was coming down the stairs to the front door, Dani rose. "I'll be on his tail in case he heads to the Underground."

"Info says he drives there," Mitch said.

"Then get ready to pick me up. I just want to see what he's like up close and personal."

"Want to use your nancy radar?" Mitch teased, but she was already heading out the door and following Williams as he walked down the block.

She crossed over and trailed him, keeping a good distance until he slipped into the small grocery store on the corner. Inside, Williams was the third person in line for coffee and she eased in behind him, accidentally bumping him as she reached past him for one of the wrapped scones in a display by the counter.

"Sorry," she said with a broad engaging smile.

Williams reciprocated the smile, displaying American-perfect teeth and full tempting lips. His eyes were a hazel-green mix, leaning more toward green. The suit he wore was definitely not off the rack. The cut and cloth were too fine.

"No problem. You're not from the neighborhood, are you?"

She stuck out her hand. "Dani Sue Williams from Battle Creek, Michigan. I'm staying at the Best Western right around the corner." She had noticed the sign the day before when they had turned onto the street for Mitch's flat.

The man behind the counter coughed to get their attention, and Williams placed his order. He seemed ready to engage her in conversation again, but the server quickly set his coffee on the counter.

Dani waited, watching as Williams paid, and when he began to walk away, she ordered her own coffee but then Williams returned and handed her a card. "In case you'll be in the area a bit," he said with a wink and walked out.

She ordered a plain coffee to avoid being delayed and when served, tossed some money on the counter, not bothering to wait for the change. Once outside, she searched the street and found Williams a block up, getting into a car. She immediately headed toward the van, but Mitch had noted Williams's actions and had already pulled out in her direction.

He stopped to pick her up and as she slid into the passenger seat, he said, "So is he gay?"

She held up his card. In blue ink on the back was his phone number.

"Damn, you're good," Mitch said and followed Williams as he pulled out.

The flight to London had been smooth. A car had been waiting for him at Gatwick to whisk him away to the Four Seasons. Contrary to the popular line, crime did pay and quite handsomely. His family had vast investments throughout the world and quite a lot of ready cash.

During the course of the night, Troy had set up his connection to their network and tapped into the video feeds from the cameras he had placed in his mother's bedroom. He fast-forwarded through the disgusting sight of Trip screwing his mother but slowed the video to normal speed when his mother shoved Trip off to answer her cell phone.

It had been her contact again, advising Cassandra that the Sparrow was on her way to London—not that he hadn't guessed that on his own already. What had come as a surprise was the information that the Sparrow had someone at SIS on her list—Jared Williams.

The Williams name was a new one, and Cassandra seemed a bit befuddled by the development.

Troy had expected her to send Trip after two of the men, Breckenridge being too prominent to attack without serious consequence. Instead, she had gotten back in bed with her assassin, a pleased and rather devious smile on her face. She had something cooking, he thought. Something she planned to unleash when the time was right.

In the meantime, he had to track down Williams. Once he did, the Sparrow would be sure to show up as well.

Chapter 24

Williams drove directly to SIS headquarters. They watched him pull into the parking area, but they couldn't linger for long without fear of detection. Instead they headed a few blocks away, and Mitch put up the dish for the parabolic listening device again.

Lucia had been able to pinpoint the general location of Williams's office for them as well as provide his phone number so they could use it to confirm they had their ears trained to the right spot. Playing with the assorted controls, Mitch managed to get a clean signal. A woman's high-pitched and slightly nasal voice was followed by a man's familiar tones.

"Sounds like Williams," Dani said.

"Let's confirm that." He dialed the number Corbett had provided, and the sound of a phone ringing came across on the signal from their listening device.

"Williams here," a man said with the same tone they had heard before.

Mitch hung up and shut off the cell phone so Williams couldn't call back or track the cell phone. Then they settled down to wait for Williams to visit someone higher up at SIS with the information possibly provided to him by someone at Lazlo. Considering the nature of the fake reports they had put out there, they didn't expect for it to take long and they were not disappointed.

Less than a half hour later, Williams's familiar voice came across the dish signal. "I've got some interesting news for you."

A crackle erupted across the line, likely the response from the person Williams had called, but it was too garbled to tell. Mitch attempted to adjust the signal to improve the reception, but it didn't help.

The garbled noise came across the phone line and then Williams said, "The Sparrow is alive."

Mitch and Dani looked at one another. It was the first piece of information they had given to one of their suspects.

More unintelligible chatter followed, but then came Williams's hasty confirmation. "I'm sure, sir. My contact has been spot on the money so far."

A long pause followed and then Williams said, "The Sparrow's on her way here, sir."

Mitch fiddled again, eager to hear the other voice on the line, but there was nothing but static.

Williams replied to the static with, "To SIS, sir. The Sparrow thinks someone here outed her to SNAKE. She's on her way here for payback."

"Bingo," Dani said. Williams had just pointed them in the direction of one of the suspects at Lazlo.

More garbled noise was followed seconds later by the

sound of William hanging up the line, but then came some more muted taps.

Mitch said, "He's dialing someone."

A moment later Williams said, "Jenkins? We have a problem."

Much as the SIS mole had apparently asked Williams earlier, Corbett now pressed them for confirmation of their report.

"You're sure about the information relayed and the call to Jenkins?" he asked

"We're sure, Corbett. But there's one easy way to find out—Williams's contact will be here tonight. At his flat."

"Chloe Winchester asked for tomorrow off. Claimed she had a family emergency," Lucia said, disgust apparent in her tones. "I can't believe it."

Chloe had been one of their suspects and was second-in-command to Lucia in the IT department.

"She fooled us all, Lucia. You shouldn't blame yourself," Corbett added, his tone surprisingly sympathetic, Mitch thought. Corbett didn't like failure or betrayal. The fact that Chloe may have been leaking info under Lucia's nose would have normally resulted in some kind of reprimand to the department head. The lack of response confused Mitch.

"If Chloe is on her way here, we can intercept her and Williams at his flat. In the meantime, do you think you can go through everything she's done to find out how she compromised Lazlo security?" Dani said.

"I've already started," Lucia confirmed. "Plus, once she steps out the door tonight, I'm overhauling security on all the systems and eliminating her access across the boards. I'll also double-check to make sure she didn't leave herself any back doors."

"That sounds like the thing to do. Will you two be able to bring in Williams and Chloe?" Corbett asked.

"Without a problem. You want them at London HQ?" Mitch asked and shot a look at Dani, who immediately added, "What about Jenkins? What should we do about him?"

The muffled sounds of a private conversation followed, but then Lazlo said, "I'm still considering what to do about Jenkins. We'll discuss it tonight once you grab Chloe and Williams."

"Will do," Dani said and after they had hung up, she looked at Mitch. "What kind of plan did you have in mind?"

He shrugged. "Easier to take them one at a time. Chloe's not a secret agent type. She spends all her time at the keyboard."

"But Williams could give us trouble. He's trained and probably armed to kill," she said and swiveled on the small stool in the van where she had been seated for the better part of the morning.

"I could take Williams inside the apartment before Chloe gets there, but we do want her to show up at his flat. That will confirm we've got the right person," he said.

Dani should have been insulted that he thought he should be the one to take Williams. She'd taken down men much bigger than Williams in the past and without the use of much force. Men always seemed surprised when a pretty face turned out to be more than they expected.

"You could take him, but I think I've got an easier way to get through the front door," she said and pulled Williams's card from her pocket.

With a resigned sigh, Mitch recognized that she was right. "You get him to open the door and I'll make sure he doesn't know what hit him."

"Deal."

* * *

Williams was a dog, like most men, Dani thought. She had called him to say she was still in the neighborhood and did he want to get together for a quick drink.

Even though Chloe Winchester was set to arrive in just a few hours, Williams had had no hesitation about inviting Dani up to his flat. Rather stupid for an SIS operative. You never took home a stranger, and even supposed friends were suspect until you cleared them.

She had investigated Mitch when they'd first met, suspicious of him even while intrigued by him. Luckily his background check had revealed he was one of the good guys, Dani thought as she sat in the passenger seat of the van and glanced up toward the light in Williams's flat.

"I'm ready if you are," she said.

"Ready." Mitch was dressed all in black with a black stocking cap on his head to hide him when he entered through the back window she would open for him. He was armed with his Heckler & Koch in a shoulder holster and a smaller Glock at his ankle.

Similarly armed, with her trusty Sigma at the small of her back and baby Glock at her ankle, she had opted for a low-cut halter blouse, whose loose folds helped hide the telltale bulge at her back. Tight faded jeans completed her ensemble along with sneakers. For all purposes, she looked much like the Battle Creek tourist she had purported to be earlier that morning.

She glanced at her watch. "On my mark, it'll be exactly seven. I'll expect you to come through the window no later than seven-ten." They had scoped out the back of the building earlier and Williams's second floor flat was easily reached from the roof of the three-season room attached to the first floor. They had guessed that the two back windows belonged to a bathroom and a bedroom.

Dani would ask to use Williams's loo and make sure the window was unlocked.

"Okay. One, two, three. It's now seven," she said.

"Seven," he confirmed and she stepped out of the van and walked up to the door of the rather elegant row home. She pressed the button for Williams's flat, and the buzz of the door release sounded a second later.

Way too sloppy, she thought, unless good ol' Jared had a camera system in place. Of course, she couldn't take the time to inspect. Once inside, she walked down the hall to a back staircase and went upstairs. Jared Williams was already waiting for her at his door, a smile on his face.

"So nice to see you again," he said and moved in quickly, pecking her on either cheek and slipping a possessive arm around her waist.

Damn, but she hadn't expected the lech to move all that fast. She hoped he didn't sense the hardness of her holster and weapon. Acting quickly, she leaned toward him, removing some of the pressure of his arm at her waist, and dropped a quick kiss on his lips. "Thanks for asking me up. It's always tough being in a new place. It makes you feel so alone," she purred sexily.

Williams walked her to the couch and motioned for her to sit, but she laced her fingers together and executed a small bounce in that universal kind of sign language that hinted at her need. "Would you mind if I used the toilet first?"

"No, of course not. Freshen up while I get us something to drink. Is wine all right?" he asked, walking away from her and to a dry bar fitted at an angle in the corner of the room.

"Wine is fine," she said and with the barest of glimpses at the flat, decided it was done in early Lounge Lizard. Williams clearly liked to think he was hot stuff and seemed prepared to entertain often. Of course, his pretty boy looks probably did help him land women to regularly share the space.

With an engaging wink in his direction, she said, "I'll go freshen up."

In the bathroom, she locked the door and pulled back the shower curtain to reveal the window. It was high on the wall and would be tight for Mitch. She reconsidered using this window, but moving to Williams's bedroom was too risky. Unlocking the window, she opened it and pulled a small flashlight from her purse. She waved it back and forth a few times and an answering wave came from below in the garden.

Satisfied that Mitch was in position, she flushed to keep up the ruse, washed her hands and returned downstairs.

Williams was sitting on the couch, one arm draped over the top of the sofa while the other held a glass of wine. As she approached, he rose and with some pomp, snared a glass from the coffee table. He walked to her, holding the glass out.

She accepted it and took a sip. "Excellent."

"I'm glad you think so. I'm also glad you decided to call." He sipped at his own drink and came to stand before her. Picking up his hand, he ran a finger along the short strands of her hair that swept across the side of her face.

"You look familiar," he said and narrowed his eyes, as if trying to place her.

Dani was certain they had never met before, but he might have seen pictures of her from the SIS files. Time for distraction. She copied his actions, running her free hand through the close-cropped strands of his sandy hair. "Some people think I look like Julia Roberts."

"Hmm. Yes, maybe that's it." He moved his hand and ran his thumb over the edges of her lips. "You have the same sexy smile."

Time passed too quickly. Mitch would enter soon and their position in the room still gave Williams a clear look up the stairs. She needed to change that. She laid a hand on his shoulder, stroked the muscles there beneath the expensive cotton of his shirt. With a step toward her left, she gently persuaded him to pivot or lose their physical connection.

"You think I'm sexy?" She stepped toward him and nuzzled his nose with hers, playfully teasing him. As she shifted the position of her head, intending to kiss him to keep up the distraction, she noticed the movement coming down the stairs.

Williams didn't.

Mitch Tasered the side of his neck and Williams dropped to the ground, his body convulsing.

She went to work, dropping to her knees and grabbing the cable ties Mitch held out to her. Efficiently she bound Williams's ankles and wrists.

"Seemed to be getting pretty cozy there," Mitch said as he hauled a stunned Williams to his feet and dragged him to a nearby dining room chair, to which he secured him with yet more cable ties. When he was done, he duct-taped Williams's mouth so that he couldn't call out.

"Just doing my job," she answered, trying not to be secretly pleased at the slightly jealous undertones in Mitch's voice.

With a peek at her watch, she said, "I guesstimate Chloe will arrive here in about two hours."

"Good. That gives us two hours to get some information," Mitch said, and as the effects of the stun gun appeared to recede, Williams's eyes widened at the sight of Mitch standing there, TEC-9 slung over his chest and Taser in hand.

Mitch pulled over another dining room chair and turned the rungs toward Williams. He sat down and laid the hand with the Taser across the top of the chair. "You know what this can do. Especially to some of your more private areas."

Williams jerked against the bindings, and muffled protests came from behind the tape. Trying to calm him, Dani said, "My friend can be a little aggressive at times, but not to worry. I can control him."

Mitch shook his head, *tsk*ing as he said, "Come on now. Just a little zap will do it."

Dani walked to Williams and pulled off just a bit of the duct tape. Williams glanced up at her, his gaze pleading, and she said, "We have a few questions. After that, we'll turn you over to the Lazlo Group and the authorities. If you cooperate, we'll make sure you're treated fairly. Understand?"

At his nod, Dani ripped off the bulk of the tape, earning a protest. "Bollocks, luv. Was that really necessary?"

"Cocky, isn't he, love," Mitch mimicked. With a push of the button on the Taser, electricity sizzled between the two posts on the hand-held device. "Good. Gives me more to work on."

Dani gave Williams some credit. He didn't flinch at Mitch's threat. Standing before their captive, she placed her hands on her hips. "Tell me something, Jared. Why Chloe?"

He smiled. "Why? Because she was needy. Horse-faced computer geek with an ax to grind. Perfect person to work."

She shot a look at Mitch, who shrugged. "I can confirm the horse-faced bit."

Dani rolled her eyes and continued. "What kind of ax?"

"She thinks Lazlo has the hots for his top computer geek and was promoting her because he was sleeping with her. Chloe thought she should have gotten the top spot in IT. Perfect for me that she hated Lazlo and wanted to get even."

"Why?" Mitch asked.

"Because so do a lot of people at SIS."

"Enough to kill five Lazlo operatives, Randy Kruger and the Sparrow?" Dani asked and placed her booted foot on the edge of William's chair. She leaned forward, braced an elbow on her knee and when he didn't answer, pressed again.

"I won't tell you who I report to," Williams said.

"You know that eventually we're going to make the connection between you, your superior and these murders. Once we do, you're going down with him unless you cooperate," she said, but Williams shook his head vehemently.

"I had nothing to do with them. All I did was provide details of high-profile Lazlo Group assignments. Nothing else."

"So what did you tell Barrett Jenkins?" Mitch said and zapped the Taser again.

"I don't know—"

Dani snagged some strands of his hair and yanked hard. "Come now, Jared. We know your old man was Jenkins's partner so don't deny knowing him."

"You fed info to your SIS superior in order to suck up to him. What did Jenkins give you in exchange?" Mitch asked.

"Jenkins was interested in different things," Williams admitted.

"Like what?" Dani pressed.

"New SIS policy developments. Any investigations involving politicos or a series of names on his very short list."

Dani straightened and paced for a moment before asking, "Any overlap in what you told your SIS superior and what you told Jenkins?"

With a shrug and a toss of his head, Williams said, "Possibly."

"This is going rather slowly," Mitch said and pushed up his sleeve theatrically to look at his watch. "Too slowly."

He rose from the chair and stood beside Williams. He

seemed immense compared to the seated man, and Williams didn't fail to notice the size difference as he trailed his gaze up Mitch's long and broad length. There was a quaver in his voice as he asked, "What else do you want to know?"

"Everything," Mitch said.

Chapter 25

Taking Chloe was a little too easy. Dani opened the door, and when Chloe stepped in and saw Mitch, her mouth dropped open. She obviously recognized him from his time with the Lazlo Group. Chloe picked up her hands and brought them together, readying them to be cuffed.

"You got me," was all she said, disappointing Dani, who had really been itching to clock the woman who was, as Mitch and Williams suggested, rather horse-faced.

Dani cuffed her with the cable ties, and after releasing the ties on Williams's ankles, they walked them down to the van where Dani and Mitch secured them in the back and drove to Lazlo headquarters, a two-story building near Carnaby Street not far from Mitch's flat.

Mitch slipped into the alley behind the building and was turning into a parking spot when they heard the squeal of tires. Before Mitch could react, Dani's side of the van was broadsided by a large black Hummer. The blow jerked her back and forth in the seat and something gave in her side..Intense pain ripped through her rib cage, so much so that she almost blacked out, but she held on, knowing she had to act.

She gripped the side of her door, trying to stay upright as the van tipped up onto two wheels. It was about to roll over when the driver of the Hummer backed up.

The van thudded back down to the ground, jarring her and eliciting an anguished moan.

"Dani, hang on."

Mitch was already popping out of the van, the TEC-9 tucked against his side, spewing bullets at the Hummer.

It took her a second to realize that the driver of the Hummer was returning fire from behind the protection of the driver-side door. Between the two front seats sat the Heckler & Koch XM-8. Mitch had loaded it with large-caliber bullets. Probably big enough to punch through the door of the Hummer.

She bent to grab the rifle, but stars danced before her eyes as pain lanced through her side, robbing her of breath. She forced herself to reach the weapon and tried to open her door, but it was too badly damaged from the impact.

Mitch continued to fire, as did the other driver, but she knew Mitch was going to have to change the clip on the assault rifle soon. He'd need backup without delay.

She smashed the butt of the XM-8 against her window and knocked out what remained of the glass that had shattered at the initial impact with the Hummer. Slipping the nose of the gun out the window, she opened fire on the Hummer's door, the fire power and caliber of the bullets so strong, doing so ripped large holes in the door and rocked it back against their assailant.

Sensing he might be overpowered, the driver of the Hummer decided retreat was best. He hopped back into the vehicle and with a squeal of the tires, tore out of the alley backwards.

Mitch likewise jumped back in and gunned the van from the alley as the sound of sirens came closer.

He shot a glance at Dani and then at their two captives, who seemed to be fine in the back of the van. "You okay?"

"Okay," she whispered. It was all she could manage now. She tucked her left arm tight against her side, trying to immobilize her body as best she could. Each jostle of the car brought renewed agony, but she couldn't let that interfere.

"Need to call Lazlo," she said, and Mitch grabbed one of the cell phones that had been sitting in the drink holders between the bucket seats.

While driving, he dialed and when someone answered he said, "We've been attacked. We need a secure location to drop off the suspects. Also, we need a doctor for Dani."

"I'm okay," she forced out, unable to draw a full breath.

"Okay, I got the address. Make sure it's really safe this time," he said.

Dani didn't get a chance to argue about her injury. As soon as they arrived, Mitch jerked open the damaged door, eased his arms beneath her legs and carried her down and through the door of the country estate to which he'd driven.

She had no doubt it was "really safe" as Mitch had asked. They had passed through a massive security gate and armed guards were at every corner of the building.

Inside, an attractive Latina woman was waiting for them. Lucia, she assumed.

"Where's Corbett?" Mitch asked.

"Taking care of some things," Lucia said. "The doctor is on his way. Why don't you take Dani upstairs? Second room on the right."

He stalked up the stairs, trying to keep her as steady as possible so he could keep her pain to a minimum. As he gently laid her on the bedspread, he ran the back of his hand across her cheek.

"I'm okay, really. I just aggravated that rib strain."

"We'll let the doctor be the judge of that. In the meantime, close your eyes and rest. I'm going to help Lucia with our guests."

She watched him go and bit her lip, fighting tears and fighting mad about the pain. They were so close to finally getting some useful information and now this.

Jared Williams and Barrett Jenkins. Chloe. The start of the connections to Jenkins and possibly to John Breckenridge and the crime syndicate. So close, and now this.

A knock came on the jamb of the door. The doctor, bag in hand.

"Come in," she said, but the words were strained and lacked any force since she could barely draw a breath.

The doctor noticed it immediately and was soon at her side, poking and probing, dragging a ragged gasp from her with one touch. She imagined that she actually felt the rib moving and when she met his gaze, he confirmed it.

"Nasty separation. I had been told you had a sprain."

"Started as a sprain. We had an accident—"

"With a weakened intercostal, any sharp movement or trauma could cause the separation," he explained. He dug around in his medical bag and whipped out a bottle of pills.

He opened it, spilled out two and handed them to her. "I'll get some water," he said, then walked to the bathroom connected to the bedroom and returned with the glass, which he handed to her.

She normally didn't take anything, but the pain was such that she didn't hesitate this time. She sat up a bit with the assistance of the doctor and downed the pills, then chased them with the water.

"There's not much I can do but tell you to rest, avoid strenuous activity and additional trauma. I'd suggest that you get a flak jacket or something similar to protect those ribs. In the meantime, I'm going to wrap them up, but I'll make sure we get you a rib belt by the morning."

"Can't wait until morning," she said, although she was already starting to feel groggy from the pills and suddenly wondered what he had given her.

"What did you—"

"Enough Percocet to get you to rest," he said and began to unbutton her shirt so he could wrap her ribs.

She reached up to stop him, but her hands only flailed futilely.

Trying to protest, she barely managed a croak as the room swirled in her vision a second before darkness claimed her.

Mitch stalked back and forth in the large conference room where he and Lucia had interrogated first Jared Williams and then Chloe Winchester. He somehow understood Williams's actions—the man was ambitious and greedy. Feeding information to an SIS superior earned him brownie points. Providing similar details to Barrett Jenkins earned him enough money for his expensive lifestyle.

Corbett had arranged for SIS to come collect Williams the next day, although given Williams's assistance to what they assumed to be an SIS deputy director, he suspected the punishment for his actions would be minimal. At worst it seemed as if Williams had provided basic information to his superior about the nature of the Lazlo operations. Williams had known nothing about the Sparrow other than what any other SIS agent would know…except of course for the information Chloe had provided earlier that day.

As for Chloe, the vitriol behind her actions astounded him. Once they had gotten her going, she had ranted and raved for close to an hour about how Corbett favored Lucia and had improperly elevated Lucia above her in the technology sector. Then she had attacked Lucia's looks, accusing her of sleeping her way to the top with Corbett, much as Williams had already told them.

When pressed Chloe confessed to passing details of Lazlo operations and their locations which explained how SNAKE had possibly known of Kruger's whereabouts.

Her need and anger was such that it was obvious how Williams had turned her. He had smooth-talked her and bedded her, leading her to believe that he actually cared about her. Williams had also promised Chloe that he would put in a good word for her at SIS. Help her secure a new job there. One where she would be appreciated.

Lazlo had immediately terminated Chloe, but he had made it known to her that whether or not he brought legal action against her would depend on how much she cooperated with them by providing complete details of what she had said and to whom.

Which left Jenkins, Breckenridge and Williams's superior and possible mole free for the moment. But even with the three still possibly on the loose, he felt immense satisfaction at finding the Lazlo leak and cutting the flow of information to Williams and his contacts. Still, Mitch itched to go after the Dumonts and connect them to the crime syndicate that had nearly killed both him and Dani.

Dani, he thought as he slowly walked up the stairs, holding the envelope that a messenger had brought for him shortly after they had ended their preliminary interrogation of Chloe.

At the door of the room, he paused and knocked lightly. No sound came from within and he cracked the door open a bit and peered inside.

Dani was still asleep in bed.

He told himself to walk away. There was no way she could continue the mission, and he wasn't ready to walk away from it. But he also wasn't ready to walk away from her.

His feet seemed to make the decision for him since he found himself moving to the side of the bed where he stood, juggling the envelope in his hand as he gazed at her. She must have sensed his presence since her eyes slowly opened, and she shot him a weak grin.

"Hi," she said.

He sat down on the edge of the bed beside her. "How's the pain?"

"What pain?" she innocently asked, and as he examined her more carefully, he noted her dilated eyes. She was as high as a kite on the pain meds the doctor had given her.

He was about to say something when the phone beside the bed rang, making Dani jump. He immediately answered and Lazlo said, "Put me on speakerphone."

Mitch hit the button and Lazlo continued. "You've done a marvelous job at unearthing Chloe's deception and the connections to SIS and Jenkins."

"We still need to do more," Mitch said, and Dani seconded it with a slightly too emphatic, "Yes, we do!"

"Ah. I see the good doctor has taken care of Dani. It's

nothing to worry about, Mitch. A costochondral separation. Painful and slow to heal, but not life threatening."

"I'm ready to continue the assignment, Corbett," Dani chimed in, her words almost singsong.

Mitch could find nothing funny about it. "I don't think Dani—"

"I'm fine, Mitch," she said and tried to rise, but not even the pain meds were enough to curtail her distress. She fell back onto the bed with a shallow gasp, all that she could manage with her injury.

"I appreciate your dedication, but I think it's time to turn the mission over to the next round of agents."

"What about Olivia Alegria?" Dani asked, her mind obviously clearing from the effects of the drugs.

"I will contact Olivia and let her know what we've learned so far. I hope that in time we can catch Sergio's killer," he said, but then quickly added, "Did you get the envelope, Mitch?"

Mitch turned the envelope over and over in his hands before Corbett said, "Well, open it, my lad."

Clearly Corbett had eyes everywhere. He tore open the envelope and removed two fake American passports and plane tickets. Open-ended round trip tickets. Destination Tahiti.

"I don't get it," he said and flashed the passport and tickets to Dani, who also demonstrated puzzlement.

"Dani is going to need several weeks of rest to heal. What better place than Tahiti? When you're both ready, you let me know what you each want to do. I've got connections with the FBI and CIA as well as several private agencies." There was a pause before he added, "Of course, I'd be delighted to have you both continue with the Lazlo Group once we've settled this problem."

Dani met Mitch's gaze. He seemed surprised when she

nodded and said, "Thanks, Corbett. I think a few weeks of rest is just what both of us will need."

"I'm glad you're being reasonable, Dani. It may take a few days before you feel well enough to travel. The estate is at your disposal. Just ask the staff for whatever you may require."

Dani realized that it wasn't just her doped-up state that had her confused about what she needed. It was Mitch, sitting beside her anxiously. Emotions alive in his gaze. A roiling mix of emotions that maybe time might help sort out. A few weeks in Tahiti might be just what they needed to settle whatever was going on between them.

"Thank you again, Corbett," she said, and Mitch echoed her thanks before hanging up.

"I don't get it. What about finishing the mission? Finding those at the crime syndicate who killed your parents?"

She heard it in his tone although he didn't ask. *What about us?*

"The rest will help me heal and get centered. Rededicate myself to what's important." She was too confused to know that anymore.

With a nod, he said, "Right. Rededicate *ourselves*."

He rose from the side of the bed and said, "Get some rest. I'll come by in the morning."

"Okay," she said and watched him go, using what little remained of her willpower to keep from asking him to stay with her. Lie beside her on the bed and comfort her when the pain meds wore off.

The pain meds were still working nicely, but not enough to stop the ache in the middle of her chest. Right smack in the area of her heart. She doubted that even a few weeks of rest in Tahiti would be enough to heal that. She didn't know if anything would ever heal that.

Could she deal with walking away from him? Could there be a way for them to work together, but not be lovers?

As she closed her eyes, she thought about how empty her heart felt with his absence. How it would feel if he walked away forever?

The time in Tahiti might help her prepare for that. It might also help her decide if letting him go was really what she wanted to do.

Chapter 26

Dani ran her hands over her twin sister, Elizabeth's, swiftly growing belly, unable to believe that in just over four months she would be an aunt.

Her sister had already been glowing when Dani and Mitch had arrived at the resort where Lazlo had taken the liberty of booking rooms. Apparently he had also sent Lizzy Bee and her newlywed husband Aidan there to keep them safe until they had gotten a handle on who was attacking the Lazlo Group.

Lizzy's joy at seeing her again filled Dani with peace as did her softly whispered words as they had held each other.

"I knew in my heart that you weren't dead."

The first few days in Tahiti had flown quickly since her battered and tired body had screamed for rest. She had spent most of those first few days sleeping, with Lizzy and Mitch constantly checking on her during her moments of recovery.

Now she had the energy to spend her first full day with her

twin sister. The two men had gone off to fish or surf or do other manly man things.

"You're happy?" she asked, rubbing her hands over the mound of Lizzy's belly.

"I am. Aidan is…wonderful," she said with a wistful sigh.

"He doesn't strike me as the kind to settle down," she said, worried for her sister and, in reality, worried for herself. Aidan and Mitch were two of a kind. During the flight down here and after, she had thought about her sister's normal life and if she could one day have the same. Whether it was time to put aside the death and violence of the past, and live for the future instead.

"I didn't think he was, but he's shown me otherwise in the past year. What about you?"

"Me?" she nearly whispered, her emotions still confused.

"Yes, you. As in you and Mitch. I can see that you care for him," Lizzy said and reached out, ran her hand through Dani's short hair. "I kind of like this."

Dani smiled and laced her fingers with her sister's. "You always want to simplify everything, Lizzy Bee."

"Love *is* simple, Dani. Don't make it more complicated than it is," she admonished, playfully shaking their joined hands.

"My life is nothing but complicated. We need to finish this assignment—"

"There's only one thing you should be worrying about."

Dani arched an eyebrow. "And what's that?"

Lizzy gestured with her head behind her and Dani half turned, her ribs protesting the movement still but better than they had been just a few days ago. Mitch and Aidan were walking toward them, holding fishing poles. Aidan also had a string of fish in his hand, which he held up for Lizzy as he neared.

"Think you can make something tasty with these?"

"I thought this was supposed to be a vacation," she teased as she took the line of fish from her newlywed husband.

Aidan wrapped his arm around her waist and hugged her hard. He laid a big hand across her belly and said, "But we're eating for two now. You wouldn't want to starve us, would you?"

Lizzy nudged him playfully and shot a look at Dani as Mitch stood there, awkwardly viewing the scene. "Let's go, Aidan. I think Dani and Mitch have things to discuss."

With a gentle bump of her hip, Lizzy urged him away toward the beach cottage where they were staying.

That left her alone with Mitch, an awkward silence stretching between them, much as it had for the entire time since Corbett had announced that their job for him had finished.

She didn't know how long they could keep it up, and in truth, she didn't want to. She'd never been a coward about anything before and wasn't about to start now. "I'm not sorry we got to work together."

"Is that all it was? Work?" he immediately challenged as he kneeled in the sand beside her beach chair.

"No. It wasn't just business. There was pleasure there as well."

It clearly wasn't enough for him. "Just pleasure?"

She remembered making love with him. The satisfaction in his arms and the comfort that followed. Lizzy had said love was simple, and maybe it was. Maybe it was all about that comfort. About the peace that came from the feel of his big body beside her during the night. The way her heart skipped a beat in the morning when he woke her with his gentle loving touch.

"When we were on the plane, you asked me who it was that

I imagined beside me in bed. Across the dinner table from me."

He seemed surprised that she remembered but clearly pleased. He leaned toward her and cupped her cheek. "I did ask you that, only—"

"I lied." Dani hesitated, but thought about the loneliness that had crept back into her life during the last few days because of his absence. She didn't want to be lonely anymore. She didn't want to waste the gift she had been given by having Mitch come back from the dead. "I lied because I was afraid you would leave again. The truth is I was afraid to tell you the truth because it would complicate the matter. It was always you I imagined beside me, almost from the day I first met you."

A broad smile came to his features, but then he quickly schooled them, as if afraid to trust in her confession too much.

"Mitch?" she pressed, needing something from him.

With a shrug, he reached down and took hold of her hand. "I've never really had a home, Dani…until I met you. You made me want things I didn't think were possible."

"Lizzy Bee says love is simple." She searched his face after she said it and wasn't disappointed with what she saw in his eyes. The few days in the sun had tanned his skin to a delicious caramel color, enhancing the light gray of them. She ached to touch his skin. Taste it. But more than that, she wanted to know she wasn't the only one who would be touching and tasting.

"I'm not a simple woman, Mitch. But being with you…"

She finally gave in to her need and laid her hand on his tanned chest, right over his heart. "Home is here, Mitch. With you. Wherever you are."

A shudder racked through his body, and he laid his hand

over hers as it rested over his heart. "I love you, Dani. Can you forgive me for not telling you I was alive?"

"I can. I'm not free from guilt either," she admitted, recalling her deceptions and her role in the prince's death. She regretted his untimely death and her role in it. Her parents would not have wanted someone to die to avenge them.

Mitch saw the shadows in her eyes and knew. "I can forgive you, but you need to forgive yourself as well. I think you know in your heart that what you did was for a good cause, even if it turned out badly."

"A good cause," she said with a huff and dropped her head as if to hide the sheen of tears there. In a choked voice, she added, "I didn't find their killers. I'm not sure I ever will."

Mitch cupped her chin and applied gentle pressure until she faced him once again. "I think the one thing your parents would want for you more than anything is that you be happy."

A tear finally slipped down her cheek. "You make me happy. I love you, Mitch. I don't want to lose you again."

He smiled, bent and kissed away the tear. Against her lips, he whispered, "I've been thinking it's time for me to settle down. Maybe find someone like Lizzy."

"Just like Lizzy, huh? I can't cook as well as she can," she said, but rubbed her lips against his.

"I may have to reconsider this deal, then."

"What deal, Mitch?"

He grinned and finally kissed her until she was breathless. After, he cradled her cheek and said, "The deal where you and I spend the rest of our lives together somewhere nice and quiet. Aidan tells me he loves Leonia. It would be nice to watch your little niece or nephew grow up."

Dani's smile broadened until it was as bright and warm as

the Tahitian sun. "You mean *our* little niece or nephew. I mean, I'm assuming that this rather unromantic deal is your way—"

He shut her up with a kiss, cupping the back of her head to keep her there until she was nearly breathless and clinging to his shoulders. "Marry me, Dani."

"I thought you'd never ask," she said, and gave herself over to his kisses again.

Cassandra paced across the room before him, her strides short and fast. High heels clicking a staccato beat on the tiled floor much like the rapid fire shots from his Glock.

Troy understood her anger. Trip had failed at his assignment, but so had he. The Sparrow and her big friend had escaped his trap. Worse off, his mother's Lazlo and SIS contacts had been compromised.

"Maman, I—"

She whirled, arms across her chest. Her lips a narrow slash of displeasure on her otherwise controlled features. "*Ferme-la,* Troy. I don't know who's the bigger screw-up. You or Trip."

"I can make things right, Maman," he began. A violent slash of her hand silenced him.

"Do you honestly think that I don't have a backup plan in place?"

He shook his head and eased back into the leather wing chair. "Backup plan?"

She advanced on him, standing right before him before bending and bringing her face close, her nose almost brushing his. "You have a lot to learn about this business, *mon fils.*"

He'd seen this side of her and normally cringed, but not today. Rising up in the chair, he said, "*Enseignez-ainsi moi.* Let me help you."

"Help me?" She straightened and ambled away, her trilling laugh chasing after her before she repeated, "*Aidez-moi?*"

She faced him, a broad smile on her features. "My entire life no one has helped me. *No one*."

Troy rose and stepped toward her, but she backed away to behind her large desk, placing the imposing piece of furniture between them. He stood before her, hands fisted at his sides because he wanted to reach out for her, but knew she wouldn't appreciate the sentiment.

"You've had *no one* because you've trusted no one. *Faites-confiance moi, Maman.* Tell me—"

"Williams and his little lady were just small pawns in a much bigger game, Troy. I've got a king in my pocket, ready to use when the time is right."

Damn her, he thought, but a grudging smile of admiration came to his face. "You always know what to do. Show *me* what to do."

Cassandra smiled. "In time, *mon fils.* In time."

Corbett smiled at the report Lucia had left on his desk. She had managed to collect quite a bit of information on Jenkins. He was certain that it was just a matter of time before they'd be able to put all the pieces together and stop the threat to the Lazlo group.

He was reviewing the last of the papers in the folder she had left when his computer pinged to let him know he had mail.

He had been expecting more from Lucia or possibly even an e-mail from Dani and Mitch. He had hoped that some time on a quiet Tahitian beach would help them resolve any doubts they had.

Facing his computer, he double-clicked on the message.

Think you know what's going on? Think again.

* * * * *

*Don't miss the next super-charged installment in the
sexy, suspenseful Mission: Impassioned continuity!*
TOP-SECRET BRIDE
*by Nina Bruhns
will be on sale in September 2007
wherever Silhouette Books are sold.*

Welcome to cowboy country...

Turn the page for a sneak preview of
TEXAS BABY
by
Kathleen O'Brien
An exciting new title from
Harlequin Superromance for everyone
who loves stories about the West.

Harlequin Superromance—
Where life and love weave together in
emotional and unforgettable ways.

CHAPTER ONE

CHASE TRANSFERRED his gaze to the road and identified a foreign spot on the horizon. A car. Almost half a mile away, where the straight, tree-lined drive met the public road. He could tell it was coming too fast, but judging the speed of a vehicle moving straight toward you was tricky.

It wasn't until it was about two hundred yards away that he realized the driver must be drunk…or crazy. Or both.

The guy was going maybe sixty. On a private drive, out here in ranch country, where kids or horses or tractors or stupid chickens might come darting out any minute, that was criminal. Chase straightened from his comfortable slouch and waved his hands.

"Slow down, you fool," he called out. He took the porch steps quickly and began walking fast down the driveway.

The car veered oddly, from one lane to another, then up onto the slight rise of the thick green spring grass. It just barely missed the fence.

"Slow down, damn it!"

He couldn't see the driver, and he didn't recognize this automobile. It was small and old, and couldn't have cost much even when it was new. It was probably white, but now it needed either a wash or a new paint job or both.

"Damn it, what's wrong with you?"

At the last minute, he had to jump away, because the idiot behind the wheel clearly wasn't going to turn to avoid a collision. He couldn't believe it. The car kept coming, finally slowing a little, but it was too late.

Still going about thirty miles an hour, it slammed into the large, white-brick pillar that marked the front boundaries of the house. The pillar wasn't going to give an inch, so the car had to. The front end folded up like a paper fan.

It seemed to take forever for the car to settle, as if the trauma happened in slow motion, reverberating from the front to the back of the car in ripples of destruction. The front windshield suddenly seemed to ice over with lethal bits of glassy frost. Then the side windows exploded.

The front driver's door wrenched open, as if the car wanted to expel its contents. Metal buckled hideously. Small pieces, like hubcaps and mirrors, skipped and ricocheted insanely across the oyster-shell driveway.

Finally, everything was still. Into the silence, a plume of steam shot up like a geyser, smelling of rust and heat. Its snake-like hiss almost smothered the low, agonized moan of the driver.

Chase's anger had disappeared. He didn't feel anything but a dull sense of disbelief. Things like this didn't happen in real life. Not in his life. Maybe the sun had actually put him to sleep....

But he was already kneeling beside the car. The driver was a woman. The frosty glass-ice of the windshield was dotted with small flecks of blood. She must have hit it with her head, because just below her hairline a red liquid was seeping out. He touched it. He tried to wipe it away before it reached her eyebrow, though, of course that made no sense at all. Her eyes were shut.

Was she conscious? Did he dare move her? Her dress was covered in glass, and the metal of the car was sticking out lethally in all the wrong places.

Then he remembered, with an intense relief, that every good medical man in the county was here, just behind the house, drinking his champagne. He found his phone and paged Trent.

The woman moaned again.

Alive, then. Thank God for that.

He saw Trent coming toward him, starting out at a lope, but quickly switching to a full run.

"Get Dr. Marchant," Chase called. "Don't bother with 911."

Trent didn't take long to assess the situation. A fraction of a second, and he began pulling out his cell phone and running toward the house.

The yelling seemed to have roused the woman. She opened her eyes. They were blue and clouded with pain and confusion.

"Chase," she said.

His breath stalled. His head pulled back. "What?"

Her only answer was another moan, and he wondered if he had imagined the word. He reached around her and put his arm behind her shoulders. She was tiny. Probably petite by nature, but surely way too thin. He could feel her shoulder blades pushing against her skin, as fragile as the wishbone in a turkey.

She seemed to have passed out, so he put his other arm under her knees and lifted her out. He tried to avoid the jagged metal, but her skirt caught on a piece and the tearing sound seemed to wake her again.

"No," she said. "Please."

"I'm just trying to help," he said. "It's going to be all right."

She seemed profoundly distressed. She wriggled in his arms, and she was so weak, like a broken bird. It made him feel too big and brutish. And intrusive. As if touching her this way, his bare hands against the warm skin behind her knees, were somehow a transgression.

He wished he could be more delicate. But he smelled gasoline, and he knew it wasn't safe to leave her here.

Finally he heard the sound of voices, as guests began to run around the side of the house, alerted by Trent. Dr. Marchant was at the front, racing toward them as if he were forty instead of seventy. Susannah was right behind him, her green dress floating around her trim legs.

"Please," the woman in his arms murmured again. She looked at him, the expression in her blue eyes lost and bewildered. He wondered if she might be on drugs. Hitting her head on the windshield might account for this unfocused, glazed look, but it couldn't explain the crazy driving.

"Please, put me down. Susannah… The wedding…"

Chase's arms tightened instinctively, and he froze in his tracks. She whimpered, and he realized he might be hurting her. "Say that again?"

"The wedding. I have to stop it."

* * * * *

Be sure to look for TEXAS BABY,
*available September 11, 2007,
as well as other fantastic Superromance titles
available in September.*

HARLEQUIN® Super Romance®

Welcome to Cowboy Country…

TEXAS BABY

by *Kathleen O'Brien*

#1441

Chase Clayton doesn't know what to think.
A beautiful stranger has just crashed his
engagement party, demanding that he not
marry because she's pregnant with his baby.
But the kicker is—he's never seen her before.

Look for TEXAS BABY and other fantastic
Superromance titles on sale September 2007.

Available wherever books are sold.

HARLEQUIN® Super Romance®

**Where life and love weave together
in emotional and unforgettable ways.**

REQUEST YOUR FREE BOOKS!

2 FREE NOVELS PLUS 2 FREE GIFTS!

Silhouette® Romantic

SUSPENSE

Sparked by Danger, Fueled by Passion!

YES! Please send me 2 FREE Silhouette® Romantic Suspense novels and my 2 FREE gifts. After receiving them, if I don't wish to receive any more books, I can return the shipping statement marked "cancel." If I don't cancel, I will receive 4 brand-new novels every month and be billed just $4.24 per book in the U.S., or $4.99 per book in Canada, plus 25¢ shipping and handling per book plus applicable taxes, if any*. That's a savings of at least 15% off the cover price! I understand that accepting the 2 free books and gifts places me under no obligation to buy anything. I can always return a shipment and cancel at any time. Even if I never buy another book from Silhouette, the two free books and gifts are mine to keep forever.

240 SDN EEX6   340 SDN EEYJ

Name	(PLEASE PRINT)
Address	Apt. #
City	State/Prov. Zip/Postal Code

Signature (if under 18, a parent or guardian must sign)

Mail to the **Silhouette Reader Service™**:
IN U.S.A.: P.O. Box 1867, Buffalo, NY 14240-1867
IN CANADA: P.O. Box 609, Fort Erie, Ontario L2A 5X3

Not valid to current Silhouette Intimate Moments subscribers.

Want to try two free books from another line?
Call 1-800-873-8635 or visit www.morefreebooks.com.

* Terms and prices subject to change without notice. NY residents add applicable sales tax. Canadian residents will be charged applicable provincial taxes and GST. This offer is limited to one order per household. All orders subject to approval. Credit or debit balances in a customer's account(s) may be offset by any other outstanding balance owed by or to the customer. Please allow 4 to 6 weeks for delivery.

Your Privacy: Silhouette is committed to protecting your privacy. Our Privacy Policy is available online at www.eHarlequin.com or upon request from the Reader Service. From time to time we make our lists of customers available to reputable firms who may have a product or service of interest to you. If you would prefer we not share your name and address, please check here. ☐

SRS07

Silhouette®

Romantic

SUSPENSE

COMING NEXT MONTH

#1479 MIRANDA'S REVENGE—Ruth Wind
Sisters of the Mountain
With the clock ticking and a murder trial on the horizon,
Miranda Rousseau has one last chance at clearing her sister's name.
But James Marquez, the tall, sexy private investigator she's hired to
solve the case, is fast becoming much more than just a colleague in
the face of danger.

#1480 TOP-SECRET BRIDE—Nina Bruhns
Mission: Impassioned
Two spies pose as husband and wife in order to uncover a potential mole
in their corporations. As they work together, each new piece of the puzzle
pulls them further into danger, and into each other's arms....

#1481 SHADOW WHISPERS—Linda Conrad
Night Guardians
She is determined to have her revenge on the Skinwalker cult. He's seeking
the truth about his family. Now they will join forces to uncover secrets long
buried...and discover a passion that could threaten their lives.

#1482 SINS OF THE STORM—Jenna Mills
Midnight Secrets
After years in hiding, Camille Fontenot returns home to solve the
mystery of her father's death. But someone doesn't want Camille
to succeed, and she must turn to an old flame for protection...while
fighting an all-consuming desire.